NO STONE UNTURNED

Also by Brandon Massey

Novels

Thunderland

Dark Corner

Within the Shadows

The Other Brother

Vicious

The Last Affair

Don't Ever Tell

Cornered

Covenant

In the Dark

Frenzied

Nana

The Quiet Ones

Collections

Twisted Tales

NO STONE UNTURNED

BRANDON MASSEY

DARK CORNER PUBLISHING

Copyright © 2022 by Brandon Massey

Dark Corner Publishing Edition: January 2022

All rights reserved. No part of this publication may be reproduced, distributed or transmitted in any form or by any means, without prior written permission.

Dark Corner Publishing

Atlanta, GA

www.darkcornerpublishing.com

Publisher's Note: This is a work of fiction. Names, characters, places, and incidents are a product of the author's imagination. Locales and public names are sometimes used for atmospheric purposes. Any resemblance to actual people, living or dead, or to businesses, companies, events, institutions, or locales is completely coincidental.

No Stone Unturned/ Brandon Massey – 1st edition

ISBN: 979-8-9854216-0-6

For devoted fathers everywhere

1

A month ago, if you had told Eric Newton that he would be worried about his adult daughter's safety, if you had said he would plan to ask her to move in with his family, as a tactic to keep her away from her shady boyfriend, he would have frowned and responded: "You've got me mixed up with someone else. I don't have any adult children."

What a difference a month could make.

On that breezy Saturday afternoon in October, Eric sat at a table on the patio of a tavern called Binge, at Atlantic Station. Atlantic Station was one of those mixed-use developments that had been thriving all over metro Atlanta, a blend of retail, dining, and high-priced condos and townhouses linked together via walkable spaces. As a long-time realtor, Eric loved seeing the local market experience yet another real estate boom, but as prices continued to climb, he sometimes wondered how anyone could afford these properties.

He checked his wristwatch, though his iPhone lay on the table next to his glass of unsweetened iced tea. He was forty-three and usually embraced the practice of using a smartphone for everything, but the watch had sentimental value. His granddad had given it to him.

The Citizen timepiece was old, but accurate. It was a quarter past two o'clock. His twenty-year-old daughter, Destiny, was fifteen minutes late.

He picked up his phone. Destiny hadn't messaged him since yesterday, when she'd confirmed she would meet him for lunch. He fired off a text to her: *I'm here at Binge. How far away are you?*

He waited to see the three little dots that would indicate she was replying, but the message box remained empty.

Sighing, he looked around the restaurant. Binge Tavern specialized in high-end bar cuisine, if there was such a thing: burgers made from grass-fed beef and topped with artisanal cheeses, free range chicken wings, street tacos, craft cocktails, beers from microbreweries. A selection of vegan dishes rounded out the menu.

Eric hadn't eaten anything all day and had been fighting to ignore the tempting aromas of food swirling around him, and as he scanned the place, he avoided looking at anyone's plate, but it was tough, because the spot was crowded. Beyond the black wrought-iron fence marking the edge of the dining area lay a sidewalk; beyond that lay one of the main streets that wove through Atlantic Station. Pedestrians and cars shuttled back and forth.

He didn't see his daughter. She still hadn't replied to his text, either.

Eric called his wife, Alyssa. She answered on the second ring. He pressed the phone against his ear and heard gleeful laughter—their two children, Elijah, and Brooklyn, probably playing a game.

"Hey," Alyssa said. "How's lunch going?"

"I think she stood me up. She ghosted me, whatever they call it these days."

"If she's not there yet, she's most likely stuck in traffic. You know how crazy things are in the city. Endless road construction, a couch dropped in the middle of the highway, maybe a flock of wild turkeys blocking the road."

"Maybe she's still mad at me," he said.

Last weekend, they'd invited Destiny to their house for dinner. She and Eric had gotten into a debate about the value of a college education. Eric argued that a degree was the golden ticket to the American dream. Destiny said the gig economy and side hustles were the future, and college was for suckers. He said she was young and would learn the truth soon. She said he was old and out of touch. Finally, Alyssa intervened like a referee and convinced them to change the subject, but blood had been drawn, and by the time Destiny left their house later that evening, Eric noticed a coolness in her gaze when she said goodnight.

Yeah, if the contest for "Dad of the Year" were a real thing with Destiny, he was lagging way behind in last place.

He had brought Destiny a small gift, as a peace offering: a hardcover edition of *Kindred,* by Octavia Butler. In a prior conversation, she mentioned she was a fan of Butler's work. The book lay on the edge of the table, wrapped in a red ribbon with a nice bow on top.

"She'll be there soon," Alyssa said. "When she does, try to relax and have fun, babe."

Alyssa was a licensed clinical psychologist, and after thirteen years of marriage, she knew him better than anyone. Sometimes, he believed she knew him better than he knew himself.

"It's her boyfriend, you know," Eric said. "He's filled her head with all kinds of nonsense. I've got to convince her to stay with us for a while, get her out of his orbit."

"The kids would enjoy having her here. I would, too. But when someone is in love . . ."

As Alyssa left her sentence unfinished, Eric glanced toward the road and saw the black, murdered-out Cadillac Escalade. Actually, he heard it first. The SUV sounded like a music festival on wheels.

The Escalade swerved to the sidewalk adjacent to the restaurant patio. The passenger door flew open as if kicked. The thunderous hip-hop music broadcast from inside boomed louder, drawing looks of annoyance from everyone in earshot.

Eric rose from his seat. A fist of tension clenched his gut.

The Escalade belonged to Clive, his daughter's boyfriend. Eric would have recognized the blacked-out SUV with the customized twenty-six-inch wheels anywhere; a blue Georgia State Panther logo adorned the rear windshield. The guy was a former student, maybe.

But everything about the situation felt wrong to Eric. Chalk it up to parental instinct.

"Gotta go," he said to Alyssa. "Talk soon."

Pocketing his phone, he started across the patio. The red-haired young woman serving his table gave him a questioning look.

"I'll be right back," Eric said, not slowing. "Hold my table, please."

He was at the edge of the patio reaching for the gate when he saw Destiny climbing out of the vehicle: she was slim, shared Eric's mahogany complexion, with ebony hair styled in shoulder-length braids. She wore a black blouse cut to display the tattoos on her toned arms, distressed jeans, and black wedge sandals.

It looked as if someone—Clive, presumably—were trying to keep her from getting out. From Eric's vantage point, he couldn't see inside the truck. But it looked as if Destiny snatched her arm away. She yelled something, raised veins standing out like cables on her neck. The music was too loud for Eric to know what she was saying, but her body language set alarm bells ringing in his thoughts.

His heart pounding, Eric arrived at the SUV as Destiny finally jerked free and bounced onto the sidewalk. She looked up at him.

Her copper-brown eyes glistened with tears. At that moment, this young woman might have been only two years old, not twenty. How many times had his other young children given him a look like that when something had gone wrong, a plea for a parent's help?

Destiny swiped the back of her hand across her eyes, and her armor was back in place.

"Sorry I'm late," she said. Although she'd told him she had lived in Atlanta all her life, she had only the faintest hint of a Georgia accent. "Traffic sucked."

"Are you okay?" he asked.

"This is the place, yeah?" She sniffled, almost angrily, and nodded toward the patio. "Let's go."

"Wait, did he hurt you?" Eric stepped toward the still-open passenger door, directly into a wall of sound.

Destiny hooked her thumb toward the restaurant and said something, but the music drowned out her voice. Besides, at that moment, Eric cared only about this guy, Clive.

Clive sat behind the wheel like a lounging lion. He wore a gigantic pair of sunglasses and an Atlanta Braves cap cocked sideways on his head. He had a burly physique draped in a sports jersey so oversized it might have been a kaftan.

He grinned at Eric and lowered the volume of the music.

"Yo, you her old man, huh?" Clive said. "Damn, y'all look just alike. Spittin' image, bruh."

Clive had a goatee bristling with gray hairs. How old was he? Destiny had never disclosed this man's age, but he had as much gray as Eric did.

It made everything about the situation worse. Unconsciously, Eric clenched his hands into fists.

"Did you hurt her?" Eric asked.

Clive's grin broadened. He shifted in his seat, slid his right hand to rest on something wedged next to him.

Eric noticed the glint of steel under his fingers. Eric wasn't a firearms expert, but he guessed it was a Glock.

Eric took a step back. He felt as if the ground had split open beneath him.

An image flashed through his mind, with lurid clarity: Clive shooting him in the gut right there in front of a hundred people and driving off while Eric bled out on the sidewalk. Men—especially, Black men like him—had been killed over lesser offenses.

"Shut the door, pops," Clive said, hand caressing the pistol. "Don't start none, won't be none."

Eric swallowed, his mouth feeling full of sour grit.

He stepped back and closed the door.

The Escalade rumbled away. Destiny touched Eric's arm carefully, as if fearful he might shatter into a thousand tiny bits.

"Can we please go inside now?" she asked.

2

Back at the patio table, Eric's hand shook so badly that when he lifted his glass of iced tea, the liquid nearly spilled over the rim.

"God, I could use a drink so bad." Destiny studied the laminated menu. "Can't you? You look like you need one, old sport."

Eric's brain felt foggy; Destiny's swirl of words hadn't fully registered. "Clive showed me his gun."

"Everyone's got a gun." She cocked an eyebrow at him. "You've been here before, yeah? What's good?"

Her nonchalance about what had happened was either a brazen attempt to change the subject, or proof that she believed such interactions were normal. From what Eric had learned about his daughter in the month since she had entered his life, he suspected both explanations might bear some truth.

He pulled in a deep breath, let it out slowly. His heartbeat decelerated as the shock wore off, but he wasn't ready to let this go.

"Has he ever used that weapon on anyone?" Eric asked.

"I'm his girl, not his PO."

"PO?"

"Parole officer." She shook her head, looking as exasperated as a parent trying to explain obvious things to a dull-witted child. "You should have asked him."

"How old is he? He's got as much gray hair as I do."

"Wow, I seriously hope you didn't invite me here to talk about *him*." Destiny rolled her eyes dramatically. "He's thirty-eight, thirty-nine. Not as old as you, Mr. Eric."

"Please, don't call me that. That makes me sound like I'm a Sunday school teacher."

"Hmph." She flashed a mischievous grin. "If the shoe fits . . ."

"Seriously, this guy, he's almost twice your age, Destiny. He's taking advantage of you."

"How do you know I'm not taking advantage of him?" She winked.

The server stopped by their table. Destiny ordered a Moscow mule and confidently produced an ID card when the server asked.

"I want it in the copper mug, too," Destiny said, as the server noted the request. "Blend it with top shelf vodka, not the house junk."

After the server had departed, Eric said, "Top shelf vodka? You don't turn twenty-one until the end of the month. Is that a fake ID?"

"You are way too uptight right now, Eric. I mean it, you should get a drink too, a real one, instead of sipping on that tea."

"Let me see it." Eric extended his hand across the table.

Destiny dropped the ID card into his palm. To Eric's untrained eyes, the fake was indistinguishable from the genuine article.

"You can get in trouble for using this." He handed it back to her.

"Like you didn't have one when you were my age. I know you used one to get in all the clubs and hang with the hotties. Don't lie."

"Who gave it to you? Clive?"

As if speaking the man's name had conjured him from the ether, the Escalade circled back to the adjacent road, bass rumbling from the speakers. The SUV lingered for a beat near the patio before rejoining traffic.

Destiny's jaws clenched, and she lowered her head, as if avoiding Eric's gaze. She tapped on her iPhone.

"He's keeping tabs on you," Eric said, in the gentlest tone he could manage. "You aren't his property, Destiny. This possessiveness of his is dangerous."

"I thought your wife was the psychologist." Destiny shot him a sharp look. "Ready for some counseling? What answers do you have about my biological mother, *Dad*?"

Eric leaned back in the chair. The server returned and placed Destiny's cocktail on the table. His daughter picked up the copper-plated mug and sipped with relish, her gaze never leaving his face.

She had asked him the one question to which he lacked a satisfactory answer. Who was her mother?

Facts: He'd learned about Destiny only because of his older sister, Valerie. Val had an *Ancestry.com* profile and had submitted her DNA sample for analysis, since she studied genealogy as a hobby. Wanting to learn about her biological family, Destiny had joined *Ancestry.com*, too. She'd been raised in a series of foster homes, gotten adopted when she was ten, and her adoptive mother had recently died of cancer. She had no records of her birth parents and craved answers.

Destiny and Val discovered on *Ancestry* that they shared a "close" family connection, with Val identified as a probable aunt. Well, Val had only one sibling: her baby brother, Eric.

When Val texted Eric a photo of Destiny, to say his jaw had hit the floor was a massive understatement. There was no denying the similarities in their appearance.

An expedited paternity test was merely a formality, but it confirmed the relationship—and Eric's life immediately became, exponentially, a lot more complicated. He was happily married and had two children with Alyssa. Brooklyn was eleven and Elijah was eight. He had been preparing to eventually deal with teenagers. Now, he had a twenty-year-old?

Sometimes, he still couldn't believe it.

As useful as *Ancestry* had been in bringing Destiny to Val and Eric, she hit a wall on the maternal side. Her mother, whoever she was, didn't have a profile listed on the service.

Naturally, Destiny had looked to Eric to fill in the blanks. He'd been forced to confess, to his utter shame, that he had no idea who her mother might be.

He would have been twenty-two years old when Destiny was conceived. He didn't know if she had been born prematurely, but he had worked out the most probable timeline, and none of it clicked with what had been going on in his life back then.

In January of that year, he'd been in a car accident. He spent over two weeks in the hospital, most of that time in a comatose state. After he regained consciousness—thankfully with no brain damage—he had moved back in with his grandmother, to recover. Then, he finished his bachelor's degree at Morehouse, got a job, and tried to build a stable life.

Back then, he wasn't "hanging with the hotties" in nightclubs and bedding women left and right; casual sex had never been his style. He had been dating a young woman before his accident, but they had broken up a few months after he recovered. When Destiny came into his life, he tracked down that old girlfriend, and she insisted that she wasn't the mother of any child of his and thought he was nuts for even asking her.

Eric literally couldn't think of anyone else. Granted, it had been over twenty years ago, and he didn't remember every detail about his life back then. Could he possibly have enjoyed some casual fling, perhaps mixed in with a bit too much alcohol, that resulted in a positive paternity test years later? It was the only plausible answer, but it didn't feel right to him. Even if it were the truth, the bottom line was that he couldn't summon a mother's name for his newfound daughter.

"Sorry," he said. "I owe you an answer. I don't have any excuses."

"Sure don't. You must have been a wild dude back then. Hit it and quit it."

"I brought you a book," he said, hopeful of changing the subject.

"I noticed." She sipped her cocktail, lifted the hardcover off the table. Her eyes warmed. "I read this one last year. On my phone, though. It's cooler to have the hardcover. Thanks."

The tone between them shifted. They ordered lunch—lemon pepper wings, all flats for her, a cobb salad for him—and they discussed some of their mutual interests. Pro basketball and football. New shows on Netflix worth binging. New spots in the city worth checking out.

It was amazing, really, to Eric. He had known his daughter barely a month, yet they had so much in common, and they easily found rapport with each other when they let go of their differences. Looking at her talking animatedly, he could imagine what she had been like as a much younger person, as an infant, a toddler, and so on, and such a sharp pang of regret twisted through his chest that it felt like a minor heart attack.

He had missed so much of her life. Her first laugh. Her first words. Her first steps. Her first day of school. The million experiences, some major, some minor, that connected a parent to a child, that wove a tapestry of memories that would resonate for the rest of their lives. She was an adult now. What did she need him for? He didn't know what he could give her, but he wanted to give her everything.

Then the Escalade circled back, music banging. A cloud passed over Destiny's eyes. Lowering her head, she picked up her phone.

"Before I got here, I discussed something with Alyssa," Eric said. "You can move in with us, Destiny. We have a fully furnished bedroom in the basement, it's like an apartment. If you ever need a break from things, a change of scenery, it's all yours. Rent free. We'd love to have you."

She lifted her head. A tear tracked down her cheek. She dabbed it away with a napkin and gave a little laugh.

"I'll think about it," she said. "Seriously, I will."

3

Sometimes when Eric put his hands on a steering wheel, his mind transported him back in time to the accident that nearly killed him.

As he climbed into his GMC Yukon Denali late that afternoon after his lunch with Destiny, he wasn't dwelling on the past. He mulled over the future: he hoped that his daughter would move in with them. He could see the road that lay ahead for her, even if she couldn't see it for herself. If she remained with her toxic boyfriend, she would never realize her potential and might get dragged into the gutter with him; move in with her family, and she had a chance to make something of her life.

He started the engine and positioned his hands on the leather-wrapped steering wheel.

Memories flooded back into his thoughts as if released by a dam, washing away all other concerns.

It was a cold, rainy night in January. He was driving his grandfather's Chevy pickup on a dark, lonely road winding along the outskirts of Grisby, the small town where he'd grown up. Kenny Rogers sang on the radio—his granddad had always been a fan of country western music and Eric hadn't bothered to change the station.

He drove without a destination in mind. Mired in grief.

The day before, they'd buried Granddad. Death had visited him without warning: a sudden heart attack when he lay down to sleep, and then he was gone.

As he drove, Eric couldn't get the image of his grandfather lying in the satin-lined casket out of his thoughts. Granddad wore his best suit, the suit he had worn to church countless times, but the man who lay in repose looked nothing like the one who had raised Eric.

The stiffness of his embalmed skin. His bald head, shiny as burnished wood. The oddness of his hands. Hands that looked so much smaller than Eric remembered.

That's not Granddad in there. That's someone else made up to look like him, and they're missing pieces of him and used spare parts from other people.

When the deer streaked into the pickup's headlights, Eric's reaction was a microsecond too late . . . and darkness crashed down like a steel curtain in his mind. The next thing he remembered was waking in a hospital bed, his head bandaged, and a young nurse gawking at him as if he'd risen from the dead . . .

With a shudder, Eric snapped back to the present. The memories receded like an ebbing sea. He realized he was clutching the steering wheel, his palms clammy as dead fish, his jaws clenched so tightly his face hurt.

The accident had occurred over two decades ago, yet the memory was as vivid as if it had happened last week.

Not for the first time, he wondered if he had experienced some lingering brain damage from the wreck that impacted his recollection of things, though his doctors had given him a clean bill of health. The only evidence that he had suffered an accident at all was the jagged scar across his forehead in the shape of a lightning bolt. Over time, it had faded, too.

But why couldn't he remember Destiny's mother?

A horn honked, startling him. A driver in a Ford Explorer was waiting for him to pull out of the parking spot, turn signal blinking.

"All right, I'm going."

Getting home took about half an hour. They lived in Roswell, a suburb north of Atlanta, in a small enclave of spacious, contemporary-style homes that had been constructed about twelve years ago. They were the original owners, too; it was the first piece of property either he or Alyssa had purchased.

He found his wife in the backyard working in the small, fenced-in garden next to the wooden deck. During the pandemic, Alyssa had spearheaded creating the garden as a teaching tool for their children and a reliable food supply. After life eventually returned to some semblance of normalcy, gardening remained a hobby of theirs.

Alyssa straightened, brushed a lock of dark, curly hair away from her face. She wore a faded Hampton University t-shirt and cut-off shorts, homebody clothes, but to Eric, she always looked primed for an *Essence* photo-shoot. She was forty-one, two years younger than Eric, and her amber skin seemed as smooth as it had been the day they had met.

Fortunately, their children had inherited Alyssa's natural good looks, too.

"Hey there," she said. "Lunch went well?"

He summarized his meeting with Destiny. He left out the part about Clive showing him his pistol. He didn't want to worry her. They already knew the guy was bad news.

"She hasn't texted me yet." He glanced at his phone. "I'm hoping she makes a decision soon. I've got so much planned for her if she accepts."

"You know that saying, babe?" Alyssa said. "Man plans; God laughs. Whatever she decides, we'll need to adapt, make the best of it."

"It's obviously the right move for her, but I don't know if she can see that." He pinched the bridge of his nose. "She keeps asking about her mother. I don't know what to tell her."

Empathy simmered in Alyssa's eyes. In the many years they had been together, her ebony eyes had taken on more depth, wisdom. He and Alyssa had been through a lot as a couple, but nothing as notable as this recent turn of events.

In his opinion, his wife's response when they discovered he had an adult daughter had qualified her for sainthood. They'd sat at the kitchen table together and had a focused discussion, Alyssa occasionally asking direct questions, but mostly listening to his rambling narrative as he tried to understand how such a thing could have happened. She concluded their talk with supportive words and a squeeze of his hand. *You were young back then, baby. These things happen every day in families. We'll make the best of it, take it one day at a time.* She was a glass half-full person. He wished he shared her optimism about things.

Throughout the rest of the evening, Eric kept checking his phone for a message from Destiny. He was tempted to follow up with her—*Hi, are you still thinking about my offer?*—but Alyssa cautioned him to give her time, space.

The next morning, they went to the United Methodist Church they attended in nearby Alpharetta. After the service ended and people congregated in the hallways, Eric ran into someone he knew from the men's ministry, Mark Deacon.

Deacon was about fifty, ex-military, and though dressed in a navy-blue suit, still looked ready to battle on the front lines. He was six feet tall, leanly muscular. His dark hair, threaded with white streaks, was shaved boot-camp short. He had deep-set, penetrating eyes that always seemed to be performing threat assessments. A prominent scar curved from his hairline to his cheek.

Deacon owned a private security firm that provided protection for the church. Eric knew he had other clients, too.

"I want to ask you something." Eric gestured for Deacon to follow him to a quiet area away from the cluttered corridor. "Where would someone get a fake ID these days?"

"Fake ID?" Deacon's thin eyebrows arched. "Where do we get everything else nowadays, brother?"

"The internet?"

"Right on." Deacon snapped his fingers. "I didn't believe it either, until I saw it for myself. Google it. Try it now."

Eric took his phone out of his pocket and typed "get fake ID" into the web browser. Google returned hundreds of results. Eric clicked on one of them.

"See there?" Deacon said. "Upload a basic headshot. Pay for the product with bitcoin. Get it in the mail within a week. I've seen the end result. Most of them are good enough to pass the scanner. They've even got the hologram."

"It's that easy?" Eric asked. "I had no idea."

"You look concerned." Deacon squinted at him. "Something going on?"

Eric hadn't yet shared the news about Destiny with any of his friends from church, including the pastor, though he had been a member for over a decade. He didn't know what he was waiting for: was there ever a good time to admit that an adult child of yours had wandered into your life?

"I could be overreacting," Eric said. "All kids do this stuff, right?"

"Did you?" Deacon's gaze pierced him.

Eric laughed off the question and thanked Deacon for the information.

After church, Eric and his family had brunch at a nearby IHOP, and then drove home. As Eric neared their house, he saw a familiar figure sitting in a rocking chair on their veranda.

"It's Big Sis!" Elijah cried with excitement.

"Is she moving in with us?" Brooklyn asked.

Eric glanced at Alyssa. His heart thudded. Alyssa reached across the seat, touched his hand.

Eric parked in the driveway and hurried to the front porch. Destiny stood. A suitcase and a backpack lay at her feet. Her eyes were glassy with tears, but she managed a weak smile.

"I was scared you'd change your mind if I texted," she said. "So, here I am. Is the door still open?"

4

The next morning, Monday, Eric and Alyssa discussed plans while getting their younger children ready for school.

Eric was going to work from home that day. He owned a real estate company with his sister, Val, that specialized in residential properties throughout metro Atlanta. Since the pandemic, he had spent a lot of time working remotely. Many prospective buyers and sellers used videoconferencing these days and would take virtual tours of properties as well. It worked out perfectly for him in this case, as he wanted to be home to help Destiny get settled in.

When she showed up yesterday, Destiny hadn't disclosed why she had decided to take him up on his offer and move in, and Eric didn't probe for answers. All that mattered to him was that she was there. He was bursting at the seams with his ideas for her. Now that she was living with them, he wanted to convince her to go to college. She had graduated from a high school in southwest Atlanta, said she had decent grades, but everyone knew that a high school diploma wasn't enough anymore to enjoy a stable career in the real world. A college degree gave her options.

"Your last chat about college didn't go well," Alyssa reminded him. "I had to separate you two. Neither of you would give an inch."

"I'll try a different approach this time," he said.

"College isn't for everyone. Heck, I'm still paying off student loans."

"But you have a career. You're a professional. She needs to prepare herself for a real job, financial stability."

"I'm not sure she'll view it that way."

"We could maybe give her a job at our firm. That would be something legit she could put on a resume, not like these side hustles or whatever she's doing."

Whenever Eric had asked Destiny about where she worked, she always had given dodgy answers. He suspected Clive had been putting money in her pocket to keep her under his thumb. Why else would she have tolerated an abusive guy almost twenty years her senior?

"You know what they say, father knows best." Alyssa gave him a wry smile.

"How wise were you at twenty? If I don't share my life experience with her, what benefit am I bringing here? I'm her father and I need to act like it."

"I think she's got her own ideas about how she wants to live her life."

As Eric was about to offer a rebuttal, Destiny entered the kitchen from the basement doorway. She was already dressed in jeans and a red blouse, her face kissed with light make-up.

"Good morning, all," she said. She patted Elijah and Brooklyn on their heads, and they swooned. To his younger kids, discovering they had a big sister was the coolest thing ever. Although even Elijah, all of eight years old, wanted to know about Destiny's mommy.

"You're up early," Eric said.

"I've always been a morning person," Destiny said. "I couldn't help but overhear you planning my future."

Alyssa cut her eyes at Eric. Eric only shrugged.

"I've got some business to handle today." Destiny popped a fresh K-cup in the coffee machine. "I'll be in and out if that's okay."

"Of course, it's okay, honey," Alyssa said. "You have a key now."

"Is there anywhere you need me to take you?" Eric asked. "Or maybe you want to use my truck?"

"Drive that behemoth?" Destiny spooned cream and sugar into her coffee cup, took a quick taste. "It's like a tank."

"That's the point. I like big and heavy rides. They make me feel safe, since my accident . . ." Eric let his words trail off, cleared his throat.

"Anyway, you can drive it if you want."

"Nah, I usually do Uber."

"If you change your mind, let me know. I'll be here all day."

"Actually, I kinda don't know *how* to drive." Destiny giggled, leaned against the counter with the mug cupped in her slender fingers. "I took some lessons a couple years back but didn't finish, never got my license."

"I can help you with that, too. There's a huge parking lot over at the community college, a couple miles away from here. It's the perfect spot for practicing."

"That would actually be pretty cool." Destiny smiled, a genuine grin, and Eric felt his heart lift.

"It's actually a good college, too." Eric winked.

"All right, that wasn't subtle at all. But I'm good, man."

"I'm going to keep trying."

"You do that."

Eric glanced at Alyssa, and he knew that she could read his thoughts. He was hopeful that this was going to work out and be a great arrangement for Destiny, for all of them, in fact.

Three days later, he realized he couldn't have been more wrong.

5

At first, Eric thought it was the sound of a television show that Destiny was watching downstairs, the volume cranked up to the max.

Around ten o'clock that Thursday night, he and Alyssa were in their master bedroom suite on the upper floor. Eric sat in a recliner, reading a paperback about small business improvement strategies. Propped up in bed with pillows, Alyssa listened to a mystery novel on her tablet, Bluetooth ear buds nestled in her ears.

Although Eric tried to focus on the text, his thoughts kept circling back to his newfound child. He felt good about his progress with her. The past few days, they had spent quality time together, one on one. He had given her a driving lesson in the parking lot of the nearby community college, and he hoped he could persuade her to enroll in classes at the same school. That weekend, he intended to take her to Grisby, where he would introduce her to his maternal grandmother. Grandma Nellie was in poor health and lived in a nursing home, and Eric wanted Destiny to meet her while his grandmother was still living.

The sound of muffled yelling derailed Eric's train of thought. It sounded like a woman and a man. His first impression was that Destiny was watching TV at some jacked-up volume, but when he heard the sharp cry, he knew that impression was wrong.

Tension pinching his heart, Eric set aside the paperback and rose from his chair. Alyssa looked up at him, pulled out her earbuds.

"Something wrong?" she asked.

Eric didn't need to answer—the shouting coming from downstairs altered Alyssa's expression. She gave him a look weighted with worry.

He hurried out of the bedroom. In the hallway, Elijah and Brooklyn huddled in the hallway at the top of the stairs, eavesdropping.

"Get back to bed," Eric said, in a tone sharper than he should have used.

"What's going on?" Brooklyn asked. "I hear a man down there."

"Is that Big Sis's boyfriend?" Elijah asked.

"I said, *back to bed*." Eric pointed down the hallway.

Shame-faced, the children slunk away to their respective bedrooms. He heard Alyssa behind him, but he did not slow down to wait for her.

The truth was, he wasn't sure what was going on, but he had his suspicions. He also had a fluttering in his stomach that made him feel as if he might vomit.

He rushed down the staircase to the first floor, rounded hallway corners like a man with his hair on fire and reached the basement door. The door was shut, but the yelling coming from downstairs was so loud that they might have had microphones clipped to their shirts broadcasting their dialogue throughout the house.

You think you all that now, huh, baby girl? Got all Hollywood livin' up in your old man's crib? Think you ain't gotta listen to me, huh?

You don't own me! I'm not your property!

Eric's blood felt as if it would burn out of him like steam. He had promised Destiny that he would give her privacy. But in a situation like this, there was no way that he could let this drama unfold without intervening.

Alyssa was literally on his heels. "We promised to give her space."

"To hell with that. I'm going down there."

He flung open the door and raced down the steps. He heard Alyssa hesitate, and then follow.

Downstairs, Eric saw what he expected to see, but it still felt surreal, as if a monster that a child swore lived in his closet had materialized in the light of day. Clive stood on the other side of the basement. He loomed over Destiny, who sat on a chair, her hands plunged in her braids as she sobbed. Clive had his hands balled into fists, and from the way that his loose-fitting shirt trailed over his waist, Eric could see the bulge of that pistol that Clive had shown him only a few days prior.

Don't start none, won't be none.

Behind Clive, the exterior door hung open to the night. For some reason, that inconsequential detail amplified Eric's anger. This rude asshole had come to his house late at night and hadn't bothered to shut the door behind him?

Clive's head ratcheted in Eric's direction. "Aw, hell naw."

"What's going on here?" Eric asked.

"Private chat, chief," Clive said, as if Eric occupied Clive's home and not the other way around. "Go on back upstairs. I gotta talk business to my baby girl here."

This close to the man in the harsh light of the basement, Eric was startled by an aspect of Clive's appearance that he had never seen before. Clive had a—what did you call it? a port wine stain?—whatever, it was a deep red splash of color on his left cheek, strikingly visible on his light brown skin. Eric might have noticed it sooner, but the last time he had seen the guy, Clive had been wearing a gigantic pair of sunglasses.

"Destiny," Eric said. "Are you all right, sweetheart?"

"I don't want to talk about it." Destiny sniffled. "Please, go."

"We only want to help," Eric said. "This guy here, he's no good for you. You know that. He's too old for you and he's trash."

Clive lifted his shirt and dragged that gun off his hip. The black metal glinted in the fluorescent light. The pistol looked bigger than Eric remembered, almost comically huge.

Behind him, he heard Alyssa draw in a sharp breath.

"Say that again, chief," Clive said. "What you call me?"

"Do I need to call the police?" Eric said, though he realized he had left his phone upstairs. "I need you to leave my house right now."

"We don't need no cops to settle our business here." Clive glowered at him.

Eric glowered back, cold sweat plastering his t-shirt to his chest.

Destiny gave him an anguished look, seeming to hate him and love him at the same time. Eric felt his heart twisting, hated the pain she was feeling, but someone needed to stand up to this guy, dammit, and as her father he was more than willing to step up and put it all on the line.

"I'm calling the police in three seconds," Alyssa said. She had edged beside Eric, and Eric could have kissed her: she'd had the presence of mind to bring her phone.

Perhaps because the remark came from Alyssa and not Eric, Clive seemed to finally grasp the gravity of the situation. He shoved the gun back into his waistband and reached for Destiny's hand.

"Let's go, baby girl," he said. "Come back to the crib with me. Let's talk about this."

But Destiny snatched her hand out of Clive's grasp. Clive balled his rejected hand into a fist and, shaking, looked as if he wanted to punch Destiny in the face. He might have done it, Eric knew, if he and Alyssa hadn't been there. He had the demeanor of a guy who wasn't afraid to use violence when things weren't going his way.

But Clive only cast a murderous glare at Eric, turned on his heel, and left the basement through the exterior door, not bothering to shut it behind him.

Eric exhaled. He quickly crossed the room, slammed the door against the night and locked it.

"Good riddance," he said.

He turned to talk to his daughter, but Destiny had retreated into her bedroom and closed the door.

Eric knocked.

"Talk to me, Destiny. What did he do to you this time, huh? What's it going to take for you to leave this asshole alone?"

"Please." Alyssa put her hand on his shoulder. "You're not helping right now."

"Am I the only one who sees how ridiculous this situation is?" he asked.

Shaking her head, Alyssa nudged Eric away from the bedroom door.

"We're here if you want to talk, honey," Alyssa said. "Specifically, *I* am here if you want to talk. No judgement, sweetheart."

Destiny didn't open the door, didn't respond to either of them. After a few minutes of fruitless waiting, Eric went upstairs, but he didn't go to bed. He went outside and stood in the driveway, a cold wind blowing around him and a drizzle wetting his skin. He was so charged up on adrenaline that he didn't feel the least bit of discomfort.

He looked around, but he didn't see Clive's Escalade parked nearby, didn't see him circling the neighborhood. If he had, he'd decided he would call the cops.

When he went back inside the house, he found Alyssa waiting for him in the hallway.

"Well?" she asked.

"He's gone," Eric said. "Did she come out of her room, say anything?"

"We need to give her space. That was a complete mess and could have been even worse."

"It's my fault? I'm not the one who pulled out a gun."

"Let's go to bed." She touched his shoulder. "We can regroup in the morning after we've all cooled off a bit."

He lay down in their bed, but sleep eluded him. All he could think about was how desperately he needed Destiny to break up with that guy. What did she see in him, anyway? If it were money, that was a problem Eric could solve. He could give her a job and she could earn her own money.

At some point, he finally drifted off to sleep. He woke the next morning at his usual time, a few minutes past six, before the alarm clock sounded.

He thought of waiting, but Destiny had told him she was an early riser. Perhaps she was already awake, and maybe she would be willing to talk.

Alyssa continued sleeping, her nightcap settled around her head like a halo. Eric climbed out of bed and crept downstairs to the basement.

Lights were on; the bedroom door was open. The bed had been neatly made, and the meager possessions that Destiny had brought with her had been removed. Her suitcase and backpack were missing.

Eric looked for a note, but he didn't find one.

His daughter was gone.

"She's probably gone back to her boyfriend," Alyssa said. Leaning against the kitchen counter, she took a small sip of her herbal tea. "He pressured her last night, as we witnessed, and she acquiesced. I worried this would happen—it's an unhealthy situation for her. I wish I'd gotten an opportunity to talk to her first."

It was about an hour after Eric had found Destiny's empty bedroom. He paced the kitchen, circling the island incessantly like a rat in a cage. Normally he would have consumed a couple of cups of coffee by then, but that morning, he didn't need any caffeine. Anxiety was a far more potent stimulant.

Was it really a little more than a month ago that he didn't even know he had an adult child? He wished—almost—that he could return to that state of blissful ignorance. But now he was invested, and there was no turning back.

For him, fatherhood meant being there for his children, no matter what. His own biological father hadn't taught him a damned thing, but his granddad had taught him, by example, what commitment to family was all about, and it didn't matter how long Destiny had been in his life. He was her dad, and he had a responsibility to her.

But he couldn't get over the idea that, somehow, he had failed her. If he'd been able to tell her about her mother, would that have made a difference?

Elijah and Brooklyn were getting ready for school. What was he going to tell them about their big sister? The kids had gotten attached to Destiny and this new development was going to crush them.

Eric felt as if his own brain were being compressed in a vise, restricting his ability to reason, to think. He could only keep running through the same points he had repeated to himself and Alyssa.

"She still hasn't responded to my texts or my voice mail." He looked at his phone for probably the fiftieth time.

"She's probably asleep now," Alyssa said. "Or, she's avoiding you. I think you need to back off and let things settle."

"If she moved back in with that jerk, that's the absolute worse move she could have made. The same guy who pulled a gun on her father?"

"She's deep in her feelings right now. It's not logical."

"I should have gotten more information about him." Eric bent his head, gripped the edge of the counter as if he could snap it in half like a cracker. "What do we know? He lives somewhere in southwest Atlanta, around Morehouse, the AUC. I lived there for years, know that area like the back of my hand."

"You're not going to look for her, Eric." Her gaze drilled into him.

"I didn't say that."

"Listen, I'm sure she's fine," Alyssa said. "You sent her a text. You called, left a voice mail. Now you need to wait. Let her contact you, in her own time."

"But what if she's in trouble? We *know* this guy is abusive. We know he's gotten physical with her. What if she's in trouble, babe?"

Alyssa didn't have a response. She set down her coffee mug, folded her arms over her chest, and looked worried, too.

When Brooklyn and Elijah came downstairs, Eric tried to put on a happy face for them, but of course, the first thing they asked about was Destiny. They had overheard the argument last night, after all.

"Is she going to come back?" Elijah asked.

"We won't ever see her again, will we?" Brooklyn said.

"Everything's going to be fine," Eric said. "Promise."

But he didn't know if that were a promise he could keep.

7

On Saturday afternoon, Eric drove to Grisby, alone. It was a trip he'd planned to take with Destiny. He needed to introduce her to her great-grandmother, Nellie Newton, the woman who had raised Eric as her own son. Grandma Nellie lived in a nursing home, and her days were numbered.

But Destiny still hadn't contacted him. He had sent her another text, late yesterday (just in case she didn't see his earlier text, he told himself), and left her another voice mail, too. In both messages he apologized for whatever she thought he had done wrong, for meddling in her relationship if that's what she believed he was doing. He asked for a simple acknowledgement that she was okay.

She hadn't responded to him. At all.

Alyssa reiterated to him that none of this was unusual, that she encountered similar situations in her counseling practice. Eric appreciated her perspective, but this wasn't some professional case. This was his child.

Grisby was about forty-five miles south of Atlanta. It was a town of about twenty thousand people, most of the residents African American. To Eric, going home felt like traveling back through time, as Grisby seemed to be suspended in the age of his childhood: on the surface, few things had changed since the days when he would cruise around town on his Huffy bicycle with his friends. Many of the same businesses he remembered lined Cowart Road, the heart of the town's modest business district. The same old houses stood in the neighborhoods. His old schools were still open, from the elementary school to the high school.

But if you looked deeper, you saw change, and it wasn't always for the better. Many of the downtown businesses from his youth had closed and never reopened; their old storefronts stood empty or were replaced by seedy enterprises such as pawn shops, title loan operations, and cheap liquor stores. Many of those old homes were boarded up or falling apart, surrounded by weed-infested lawns and abandoned vehicles. And whenever he passed his old schools, he saw patrol cars parked out front; police officers wandered the hallways as often as faculty.

Curious, Eric had recently checked home values in Grisby, and found the city clearly suffered from a lack of commerce and investment. Most folks living there who managed to keep their heads above water worked in Atlanta. Employment prospects in Grisby were dismal at best.

But he and his sister kept the family home. His grandma wouldn't have allowed them to sell it, though the value hadn't budged in over a decade.

At one o'clock, Eric pulled into the parking lot of the nursing home —known these days as a "skilled nursing facility." It was a sprawling one-story building, with white Hardieplank siding, green trim, and attractive landscaping. The facility was called Golden Day, a name intended to soothe, but Eric didn't find anything comforting about visiting this place. In his grimmer moments, he thought that people living there were like prisoners on death row, waiting for their number to be called.

He signed in at the front desk and headed toward his grandmother's room in the east wing. As he neared the doorway, he saw his big sister, Val, emerge from the room.

Val was three years older than he was, and at five-ten, nearly as tall. She had played basketball in high school and was good enough to win a scholarship to Grambling State. With her ex-husband, she'd had a daughter, Jalen, who happened to be a year younger than Destiny. Jalen attended Georgia State full-time and worked at their realtor office a few hours a week.

Eric had hoped to guide Destiny onto a similar path, but look how that had worked out.

"I didn't know you'd be here," he said.

"Didn't know you'd be here either, Buzz."

"Buzz" was a family nickname, coined by his granddad for reasons that Eric had never determined. Had a fly been buzzing around his grandfather's head the first time he had held Eric in his arms? No one knew for sure, but the name had stuck, though Val and Grandma Nellie were the only ones who ever used it anymore. Hearing it made Eric feel like a kid again, but at his age that wasn't necessarily a bad thing.

"How's everything in there?" Eric hooked a thumb toward his grandma's room. Grandma Nellie had good days and bad days. He wanted to know what he might be walking into this time.

"She's lucid, for now," Val said. "Have you gotten any word from Destiny?"

Last night, Eric had filled in his sister on what had happened. She was sympathetic, but she tended to side with Alyssa, cautioned him to give Destiny space and let her respond in her own time.

"No, but listen, I don't trust this asshole, Clive," Eric said. "You've never met him, Val. He's bad news."

"But she loves him, or thinks she does." Val offered a sad smile. "To be twenty again, right?"

"I've thought about finding out where he lives, stopping by to check on her."

"Which is exactly what you shouldn't do." Val touched his shoulder. "Chin up, Buzz. Things will be ok."

"Where are you going now? Are you stopping by the old house?"

"I'm going back to ATL to sling some real estate." She glanced at her phone. "I've got a six-bedroom house to show at four o'clock in Sandy Springs. One of us has to keep on the lights in that business of ours."

He laughed. "If Destiny contacts you, please—"

"Will be sure to let you know." Val gave him a peck on the cheek. "Go in and see our grandma, Buzz. She's been asking about you. You know you've always been her favorite."

8

Eric stepped into his grandmother's private room. Afternoon sunshine filtered through the half-open blinds, leaving part of the room cloaked in shadows. The air smelled of pine disinfectant, a scent Eric had always associated with hospitals and other places of pain and suffering.

His grandmother lay in bed, the mattress raised to a forty-five-degree angle. An intricately detailed quilt that she had made herself many years ago lay across her chest.

Eric cleared his throat. "Hey, Grandma. It's me, Buzz."

She didn't stir, didn't look his way. Her attention was fixed on the TV screen hanging on the opposite wall. An old episode of *The Jeffersons* was running. It had always been one of her favorite shows.

Grandma Nellie was ninety-one years old. For much of her life, from what Eric recalled, she had always looked younger than her age, but that changed with the stroke that dropped her six months ago, blacking out a significant portion of the left side of her brain.

Overnight, she had aged thirty years. The stroke stole her vitality, her mobility, her ability to form coherent sentences without a mighty struggle. Rehabilitation efforts had edged her away from the brink of total incapacitation, but her progress had waned.

Seeing her in this condition, with no real hope of recovery, was heartbreaking. Still, Eric was committed to visiting her at least once a week.

She was the entire mother he had ever known. His birth mother had died in a car accident when he was two. His biological father (he and his mom had never married) had floated in and out of his life for a short while afterward, but ultimately bailed and started a new life out in California. Eric hadn't talked to the man in thirty-five years and considered his late granddad to be his true father.

"I brought you a gift, Grandma." Eric raised the glossy bag of Lindor milk chocolate truffles he had brought, one of his grandmother's guilty pleasures. "I got the milk chocolates, your favorites."

Grandma Nellie didn't stir. Eric sighed. Val had said that she was lucid, but her state could change without warning. Possibly, talking to his sister earlier had worn her out.

Eric placed the bag of treats on the nearby table and settled into the armchair beside the bed. The chair was positioned on the left side of the bed, angled so that his grandma could see him without needing to turn.

He reached for her left hand; her right hand, damaged by the stroke, lay coiled in her lap like a dead claw. Her oak-brown skin was dry as a withered leaf, her fingers so frail it was like holding hands with a skeleton. But she squeezed his hand back, slightly, and that was something.

He sat with her in silence, periodically glancing at the television.

"Where's that . . . that . . . daughter of . . . of . . . yours?" Grandma Nellie suddenly asked. Her words were slurred. Chronic aphasia was another lingering symptom of her stroke.

Eric sat up straight. Grandma Nellie's chestnut-brown eyes shone. It was as if a switch had been flipped, powering her on.

"I was hopin' to . . . hopin' to see . . . her," she finished.

"I thought you were ignoring me." Eric smiled. "I've been sitting in here for ten minutes."

"You . . . you . . . you wasn't . . . talkin'," Grandma said. "Sittin' . . . sittin' . . . sittin' there like you . . . gone . . . sleep . . ."

"I know Val was here earlier. I won't stay long. I know you're probably tired."

"Hmph." Although the right side of her face drooped, the left side furrowed in a scowl. "You ain't . . . ain't answer . . . my question, boy. Where . . . that . . . that . . . girl?"

"I'm sorry." It was tough to meet her hopeful gaze. "Maybe I'll bring her next time, Grandma."

"Somethin' . . . wrong . . . ain't it, Buzz?" As ever, she could read him as easily as a teleprompter.

"I don't know where she is right now." Eric looked at his phone, as if a message from Destiny might suddenly appear at that moment.

"Oh." The light in her eyes faded. She looked at the television again, burrowed back into silence.

Eric knotted his hands. Earlier in the week, he had called his grandma on the phone and promised he was bringing Destiny to see her that weekend. Why had he done such a thing? In his grandmother's condition, hope was a delicate thing, fragile as a baby bird, and he had let her down in his eagerness to unite everyone.

He started talking about his other children. He showed her some recent photos of them on his iPhone. She looked at them with mild interest, not speaking. She yawned.

It was time for him to leave. When visiting, he rarely stayed more than a half hour. It took an enormous effort from his grandmother to focus on a visitor for a prolonged length of time.

"I'm going to head out." He kissed her forehead. "I'll be back to see you next week, okay?"

"You bring that . . . that . . . that daughter . . . 'fore I check out . . . of here." Her eyes were steel.

"You aren't checking out of here anytime soon," Eric said. "You're hanging on, Grandma."

She waved off his words. "You . . . you . . . you . . . bring her . . . to see me . . . when . . . when . . . you find her, Buzz. You . . . hear me?"

And Eric knew, right then, exactly what he was going to do next.

He squeezed her hand.

"Yes, ma'am."

9

"Eric, wait! Can I have a moment, please?"

Eric was heading toward the building's exit when the woman called his name, and he knew her identity before he turned around. He wanted to keep walking and act as if he hadn't heard her, but Grandma Nellie had raised him never to be rude. Suppressing a groan, he turned and gave her a smile he didn't feel like offering.

It was Michelle Cannon. He had gone to school with Michelle in Grisby; she was a couple of years ahead of him. In his hometown, the Cannon family was enormous, a vast tribe of uncles, aunts, and cousins that you seemed to always bump into somewhere.

The Cannons were entrepreneurs, and had a virtual monopoly on certain industries, at least locally. They owned several skilled nursing facilities in the area, including Golden Day. They owned a funeral home, too—heck, the Cannons had embalmed and buried Eric's grandfather, and probably the deceased members of every Black family in Grisby.

Michelle strutted toward him, high heels clicking across tile. She was a good-looking, tall, slender woman with dark eyes and an oval face that reminded Eric of a cat. An amber-colored weave flowed down to her narrow shoulders. She wore a stylish orange pantsuit with a yellow turtleneck. A platinum Cuban link chain encircled her neck, a three-carat ring glimmering on her finger, the offering from her third or fourth husband—Eric knew only she had been married several times.

Despite her outward attractiveness, he'd always felt on edge around her. There was an intensity to her gaze that made him feel as if she wanted to pin him to the floor and consume him in little bites, like a feline picking apart a mouse.

But Michelle was in charge at Golden Day, and as the lead administrator, she could determine the quality of care that a resident received and if meals were served hot or cold—or not at all. It would have been unwise to cross her.

"What's up?" he asked.

She slid toward him, invading his personal space, the fragrance of her expensive perfume clouding his orbit. Involuntarily, he took a step backward.

"Has your family come to a decision about your grandmother's remains?" Michelle asked. She spoke in a sugar-coated voice that was borderline seductive. She flipped open a binder as if ready to draw up a contract on the spot, which probably, she was.

Ever since they had brought Grandma Nellie to the nursing home, Michelle had been pestering him, and Val, about donating his grandmother's remains. He figured the Cannons made some money from doing so—the family clearly had a knack for finance—but he thought it in especially poor taste to focus so much on such a thing while his grandmother was still alive.

"We'll cross that bridge when we get to it," Eric said.

"And funeral services?" Michelle asked. "I know your people don't do cremations. You'll want a burial. We've got a limited time offer on caskets and headstones, Eric, fifteen percent off if you act now."

Eric's family had already purchased a plot for his grandmother in a nearby cemetery (which the Cannons also owned), next to his granddad. But buying the plot was only the beginning. There were myriad other considerations. Eric simply didn't want to consider them at that moment.

"I'll let you know when we're ready for that," he said. "I'll have to talk it over with Val."

"All we require is a one-hundred-dollar deposit." Michelle smiled, displaying teeth so white they must have been cosmetically brightened. She gave him that direct stare of hers as if willing him to go along with her plan, and he had to break eye contact and shake his head.

Good Lord, she's like a furniture salesperson. What's wrong with these people?

"Are you in, honey?" She stepped again into his personal zone.

"I really need to get back to Atlanta." He made a show of checking his watch. "We'll discuss this some other time."

"I'll call you next week," Michelle said, and he knew she meant it.

Eric hurried out of there and got in his truck. Originally, he had planned to visit Grandma Nellie, and then visit the family house to check on things. But his grandmother had planted a seed in his mind that he couldn't ignore.

He was going to Atlanta to find his daughter.

10

Although it was a Saturday afternoon, Eric hit a wall of slow-moving traffic on the northbound side of I-75. The electronic message board above the highway warned of an accident ahead and delays of up to forty-two minutes.

Frequent traffic jams were a fact of life in metro Atlanta and usually raised Eric's blood pressure. This time, he didn't mind the delay. It gave him time to ponder his next move.

To find Destiny, he needed to find Clive.

The only reasonable assumption was that Destiny had moved back in with the loser. But Eric didn't know Clive's last name or exact address. He knew only the general location that Destiny had casually mentioned in a conversation: Clive lived in the West End section of Atlanta, somewhere "near the park, not far from the AUC."

Eric's alma mater, Morehouse College, was located in the same area, as part of the Atlanta University Center (AUC) that included Spelman, Clark Atlanta, and Morris Brown. If Clive truly lived in that neighborhood, Eric was confident he could track him down.

Traffic didn't ease until the Atlanta skyline came into view; the buildings crowned with cumulus clouds. Eric floored the accelerator, hopped onto I-20 West for a couple of miles, and then swung onto the exit for Lowery Boulevard, one of the main arteries running through the West End.

Located a few miles southwest of downtown, the West End was one of the city's oldest historic districts. It still boasted a healthy number of classic homes, primarily Queen Anne and Folk Victorians, and Craftsman bungalows, the stately homes standing on quaint, tree-lined streets.

Nevertheless, things had changed since his Morehouse days. The mortgage crisis of 2008 had hit the West End hard, and many long-term residents had lost their homes to foreclosure. The district was experiencing a recovery, but the faces of the current residents often looked different than the people Eric remembered from back in the day.

There were two notable parks in the neighborhood close to the colleges. Eric decided to start with West End Park.

Driving as slowly as he could without inciting the drivers behind him to road rage, he rolled down Oak Street, peering at every house he passed.

Clive owned a blacked-out Cadillac Escalade. It was a striking vehicle. If he were parked within view at one of these houses, Eric would see it.

As he cruised, his cell phone rang. A photo of Alyssa popped up on the vehicle's Infotainment display in the center of the dashboard.

He considered not answering because he knew she would disapprove of his plan—but years of a faithful marriage made pressing the button to accept the call an automatic reflex.

"When are you going to be headed back this way?" she asked. "I was hoping you could pick up a couple of things from Publix."

"Umm, in an hour, maybe?"

"Is everything okay? You sound distracted."

He expelled a long breath. He could never hide anything from her.

"I'm looking for Clive's house," he said.

Alyssa was silent for a beat. Although it wasn't a FaceTime call, he could imagine her disapproving frown.

"I knew you would do this," she said. "Even though I don't agree with it."

"I only want to make sure she's okay. I'm not planning to challenge the guy to a duel."

"How the heck are you going to find his house? I didn't think she gave us his address."

Eric reached a stop sign, made a left-hand turn. He found himself on another residential street crowded with older homes; many of the houses were in various stages of renovation, gigantic dumpsters heaped with demolition refuse sitting in the driveways.

"Process of elimination," he said. "I know the general vicinity."

"Please be careful. Promise me you'll back down if this guy pushes your buttons, okay?"

"I'm only going to talk to him."

"Promise me, Eric."

"Promise. I'll call you later." He ended the call.

He reached the end of the block. He was about two blocks away from the park. He needed to circle closer. She had said they lived "close to the park" so Eric needed to eliminate all residences within the park's immediate area before he branched outward.

He made a left turn, another left. Head swiveling from one side to the next. Surveying vehicles parked in driveways, under carports, and on the street.

"If he's parked in a garage, this is pointless," Eric muttered.

But then he remembered that Clive drove the extended version of the Escalade—an SUV that was so damned big it was tough to squeeze inside a standard-size garage. Chances were, if Clive were home, his SUV would be parked somewhere outdoors within view.

He was about to make another left turn to check the east side of the park, when he saw a hulking black vehicle parked on a downward-angled slope, in a driveway next to a duplex with white clapboard siding. He tapped the brakes.

Someone behind him honked. Eric steered to the side of the road, parked.

His palms were sweaty. He meant what he had told his wife. He didn't want a confrontation with Clive, a man who already had flashed his pistol at him twice. But what if Clive wanted a confrontation with *him*?

Don't start none, won't be none.

"Screw it." Eric grabbed his phone and got out. He stepped onto the sidewalk and headed back toward the duplex.

When he reached the house of interest, his palms dampened. The SUV parked in the driveway was a murdered-out Escalade with a

Georgia State University logo, a blue panther, adorning the rear windshield.

It was Clive's ride, all right.

Eric sucked in a deep breath and started toward the house.

11

Two doors fronted the duplex, one on the left, one on the right. At first, Eric couldn't be sure which side belonged to Clive. He stood on the front stoop facing the doors like a contestant in a game show.

Which one will you choose? Door number one? Or door number two?

He noticed a trio of small houseplants decorated the front window of the unit on the left. Once, Destiny had shared her interest in gardening, had said she'd like to spend some time in their backyard garden and perhaps cultivate something of her own. On a hunch, Eric stepped to the door on the left and knocked.

A minute passed, with no answer. Eric knocked again, harder.

The door creaked open. A towering, thin, twenty-something Black man with a longish head loomed in the doorway; his sheer, gangly length reminded Eric of a giant praying mantis. He wore a Georgia State basketball jersey, ripped up jeans, and Air Jordan flip flops. A set of gaming headphones—Eric recognized them because Brooklyn wanted the same ones—hung around his long, narrow neck, tinny sounds crackling from the speakers.

"We aren't buying anything," the guy said. "We're not coming to your church, neither."

He started to shut the door. Eric stuck out his foot, wedging the door open.

"I'm Destiny's father," he said. "I'm looking for her. Is she here?"

"Oh." Recognition flashed in the young man's sienna-brown eyes. "Dude, I thought she moved in with you. I haven't seen her in like a week."

Eric felt hope shrink like a popped balloon in his chest.

"I thought she would have come here yesterday, for sure," Eric said.

"Nope. Sorry, dude."

He began to shut the door, but Eric didn't move his foot.

"Do you have any idea where she might've gone?" Eric asked. "Any idea where she worked, or maybe friends she might be staying with?"

"I stayed out of her business. She stayed out of mine. That thing between her and Pops . . . whatever, that's their stuff."

"Clive is your father?" Eric could see a faint resemblance between the two of them. "What's your name, son?"

"Junior."

"Junior, can I talk to your father?"

"Pops is out."

Did this kid think he had come down with the last drop of rain? Why was he covering for his dad?

"I see his Escalade parked right over there." Eric pointed. "Please, I need to speak to him. I need to find my daughter."

"Yo, I said he's out. Step off."

Junior went to shut the door again, right on Eric's foot. Eric pressed his hand against the wood, keeping the door open.

"Hey, man," Junior said. "You got a problem?"

"Where did your dad go? I know my daughter is with him."

"You're way outta line, old man." Junior's lips twisted into an ugly scowl. At that moment, he looked more like Clive than ever. "I'm telling you one more time to get gone. Do I gotta bring out the crew and handle this?"

Junior pulled the door open wide. Eric saw, in the shadows behind him, the enormous shapes of two other young men shuffling toward the doorway, like giants awaking from a long slumber. Were they Clive's other sons? Junior's friends? Regardless, three-on-one weren't favorable odds for Eric.

"I'll pay you," Eric said. He didn't know where the idea came from because he had never bribed anyone in his life. But he hauled his wallet out of his pocket, grateful that he carried at least a minimal amount of cash on his person. He fished out a twenty-dollar bill and held it up.

"Tell me where your father is, and it's yours," Eric said.

"Hold up, hold up." Junior raised his hand, and the men behind him retreated into the shadows. "Is that a twenty?"

"It's all yours if you answer my question."

"What am I supposed to do with . . . with *that*?" The kid stared at the bill as if it were an ancient artifact. He let out a surprisingly high-pitched laugh that didn't fit his imposing appearance at all. "Damn, dude! Have you ever heard of Cash App?"

It wasn't often that Eric felt old, but he certainly felt his age then. The kid smiled at Eric as if Eric had been slumbering for the past two decades like Rip van Winkle.

"Fine, whatever works for you." Eric pulled out his phone and located the rarely touched icon buried deep in his collection of apps. Fortunately, the app didn't ask him to remember a password to log in, or else he would have been adrift. "Who do I need to pay? What's your handle or whatever it's called?"

"Money to blow," Junior said, and spelled it out. "And look, make it fifty."

"You expect me to pay you fifty dollars?" Eric glared at him.

"You wanna know or not?" The kid glared back. "Fifty is the price."

Jesus, I'm getting hustled here. But he submitted a request to pay the kid what he asked for, and within seconds, heard the jingle on the kid's phone confirming that the transaction was successful.

"Pleasure doing business with you, mister." Junior grinned, showing a mouthful of braces. "Okay, check it out. Somebody in a white Navigator scooped up Pops last night, like around ten. Pops said he was hooking up with a new connect to set up some business. Something major."

"Did you see anyone that you recognized in the Navigator?" Eric asked. "Someone who might've been my daughter?"

He was still banking on a delicate thread of hope. But Junior shook his head.

"It was too dark for me to see, mister," he said.

"Where did your father say he was going?"

"Grisby." The kid's large Adam's apple bobbed. "I remember that. Pops said he was going to Grisby."

Eric felt as if a bolt of lightning had struck him where he stood right there on the porch. Grisby? His hometown?

"So, we're clear," Eric said. "You mean Grisby, the town south of Atlanta?"

"Haven't you heard of it? I mean, I haven't been there either, but yeah, man. *Grisby.*"

"What kind of business did he have in Grisby?" Eric asked.

"I don't ask him his business. I'm in college, mister. Senior year. I'm not trying to follow in his footsteps, whatever."

In other words, Junior knew his old man was shady and wanted to chart a different course for his life. Good for him.

"But he left last night, you said," Eric said. "When is he coming back?"

"Haven't heard." Worry furrowed his brow. "Sort of weird, not hearing from him. I texted him earlier and he didn't text back."

"Can you give me your dad's number?" Eric asked.

"Hell, naw, and you can't buy it, either. I probably told you too much already and he's gonna be mad at me. Bye, Felisha. We're done."

Junior started to shut the door.

"Is there anything else you can tell me?" Eric said. "Please, anything at all? I've gotta find my daughter."

"Destiny actually owed me fifty bucks." He winked. "Tell her, we're good now."

He slammed the door in Eric's face.

Eric started to knock again, but held back. He had more information than he'd possessed previously, and the kid didn't seem open to sharing anything else.

Pops said he was going to Grisby.

It was perhaps the most stunning revelation thus far. What the heck could Clive be doing in Grisby of all places? Grisby wasn't some major metropolis. It was a sleepy Southern town with zero appeal to tourists and businesses. Nothing noteworthy ever happened there.

The discovery didn't feel like a coincidence, but he had no idea what it meant and if any of it was connected to his child.

As Eric walked away from the house, inspiration struck again. He stepped over to the driveway where Clive's Escalade was parked. Quickly, feeling as if he were committing a crime, he snapped a photo of the license plate.

It might prove useful later, though so far, he wasn't sure what he would do with it. It wasn't as if he could call in a favor to a contact at the DMV and run Clive's plates.

But, he suddenly remembered in a flash, he knew someone who might be able to help.

12

Angel and Lorenzo Cannon always worked the night shift.

Working the night shift required driving, and as usual, Lorenzo drove. He guided the pristine white Lincoln Navigator along Georgia State Route 155, heading into the city of McDonough, in Henry County. It was about a thirty-minute drive from their family's headquarters in Grisby.

But they had dealings in McDonough, too. The Cannon family owned a nursing home there.

It was seven minutes past eleven o'clock on that Saturday night, but Lorenzo was fully alert. He liked to be prepared, especially on nights such as that one. He had tossed back two shots of Five Hour Energy and pumped iron before he left the house to start his shift.

His partner and cousin, Angel, sat in the passenger seat, her attention focused on her iPhone. Like him, she wore maroon hospital scrubs. Unlike him, she was a true healthcare professional, a certified nurse.

Although they were blood relatives, they didn't share much in common physically. Lorenzo was in his twenties, six-foot-two and two hundred and twenty-five pounds of muscle; he had a short haircut, a mahogany complexion, a strong jawline, and thick eyebrows—he was a man with memorable features, as Mama liked to say. In her early thirties, Angel was barely five feet tall, petite, and brown-skinned with lustrous auburn hair that flowed to her shoulders; she had a heart-shaped face and heavy-lidded eyes that made her look as if she were on the verge of falling asleep into a pleasant dream. Her diminutive appearance put people at ease, gave her a remarkable bedside manner that Lorenzo often envied.

As they traveled, they listened to songs from his Spotify playlist. He preferred classic soul from the sixties and seventies—*real music*. Actual singing without electronic assistance, and people skillfully playing real instruments: drums, horns, guitars, pianos. Current music, with its autotune-enhanced singers and musically incompetent producers manipulating computers, was the equivalent of plant-based products masquerading as "meat," when anyone with proper taste knew it was fit only for the Delete button.

Mama often said he was a young man with an old soul. It was a compliment, and he tended to agree with her.

Nodding his head to the stirring sounds of Otis Redding, he lowered the volume a few notches and tried to initiate a conversation with his cousin.

"Trivia time," he said. "Who was the lead singer for The Miracles?"

Angel didn't look away from her iPhone. She was always on YouTube or TikTok and was obsessed with cat videos. She would giggle and grin at the screen as if in her own world, and Lorenzo supposed she was.

"Cousin Angel?" he said again. "The lead singer for The Miracles? Who was it?"

She looked up at him as if he'd said something in an ancient, forgotten tongue. "Huh?"

"Smokey Robinson," he said. "What was Smokey's government name?"

Angel shook her head.

"William Robinson," Lorenzo said. "Hey, another one. This one's easy. Berry Gordy founded Motown, but before he did that, he was a pro athlete. What sport did he compete in?"

"You know I don't watch sports," Angel said. She spoke in a soft voice, nearly a whisper.

"He was a boxer!" Lorenzo clapped his hands. "Isn't that something? You didn't know that, did you?"

"Boxing is dumb," Angel said. "People hurting each other for a sport. It causes so much pain. It makes me sad."

"Yeah, boxing is dangerous," Lorenzo said. "But you know, I could have been a pro boxer if Mama had let me keep competing. You remember I trained a lot and had some amateur fights? I never lost, in eight bouts. Not once. They called me Lorenzo the Lion, remember?"

Angel didn't say anything. She swiped the phone's screen with her tiny finger.

"I still like to train," Lorenzo said. "I'm young, you know. I could still have a career in the sweet science, some day. Floyd Mayweather was competing in bouts well into his forties."

Angel remained silent. He didn't mind. He liked having someone to talk to about these interests of his. Mama would not have tolerated such conversation. She would have called it "inane and uncouth," which was about the worst insult Mama ever uttered to anyone.

Mama had different plans for Lorenzo's life. She wanted him to lead the family empire someday. She was grooming him for greatness.

He accepted her guidance because she was his mother and was wise and strong, but that didn't mean he had to defer his daydreams of golden gloves glory.

"One last question," Lorenzo said, "and I promise, you'll know this one. Who was the best-known singer from the Supremes?"

Angel didn't respond right away, but her finger paused over her phone's display, so Lorenzo figured she was contemplating her response.

"Diana Ross?" she asked.

"There's hope for you, yet, cousin." He tried to give Angel a fist bump, but she only looked at his hand as if he were a leper.

Lorenzo cranked up his music again. It was a Stevie Wonder song, "I Was Made to Love Her." Lorenzo sang along with Stevie. How could you not love a song like that in favor of mumble rap or whatever the hell it was called?

Soon, they arrived at their destination: Sunrise Manor. The facility was a one-story brick building sitting on a couple of acres of freshly mown grass, flanked by flowers and shrubs. Lights glowed in the parking lot; it was empty except for a handful of essential staff.

Lorenzo and Angel had arrived long after official visiting hours had ended.

He parked the Lincoln at the back of the facility, in front of an access door typically used for deliveries. He sent a text message on his phone.

He got a reply within thirty seconds.

"We're all set," Lorenzo said to Angel. "We have twenty minutes."

Without a word, Angel picked up the black leather doctor's bag that rested between her legs and hopped out of the vehicle.

Lorenzo set the timer on his phone, and climbed out, too. For these kinds of tasks, he mostly followed Angel's lead.

The most important element was timing. They had a narrow window of opportunity available to complete their work.

After hours, the back entrance required a passcode. Standing in the bright light cast by a flood light overhead, Lorenzo entered the six-digit code. The door beeped, and they were in.

They hurried through the dimly lit storage area, opened another door, and arrived in the main corridor that connected residents' rooms.

"God's waiting rooms," Lorenzo liked to call them, because everyone living in this nursing home was literally just waiting to die.

Although a member of the Cannon family was on duty at the front desk—a requirement for these special visits—Lorenzo and Angel didn't swing by to visit. Their family member, another cousin, knew they were on the premises, because Lorenzo had texted her upon their arrival. She confirmed the rest of the staff was on break.

Lorenzo and Angel went to work.

They visited Mr. James Tolbert in room 13.

Room 13 was a short walk from the rear entrance. He had been moved to this room only yesterday, probably against his wishes. Lorenzo knew that ailing people could get attached and ornery when they were disrupted, but the order had come from on high to move him, and that was what they did.

No cameras filmed visitors to room 13. The doorway and adjacent hallway lay outside the watching eyes of their surveillance equipment.

Although it was late, when Lorenzo entered the room, he found Mr. Tolbert awake in his bed. The room was darkened, the only light coming from the television screen. The old man was watching a rerun of *Sanford and Son.*

"Good evening, Mr. Tolbert," Lorenzo said. It was important to be polite, even during such visits, and to avoid causing distress.

Mr. Tolbert was eighty-three years old according to his file, suffering from inoperable cancer. To add insult to injury, he was a diabetic and both of his legs had been amputated about a year ago.

"What you doin' up in here?" Tolbert asked. He pushed up his bifocals on his hawkish nose.

"We're here for your care, sir," Angel said in dulcet tones. She had the sweetest voice when interacting with patients, really a fantastic bedside manner. Lorenzo envied that about her.

Lorenzo shut the door behind them. You needed a staff key to lock the door; he had such a key, and quickly applied the lock.

Angel switched on the overhead dimmer lights, adjusting them so they were just bright enough for the two of them to work without fumbling about. Mr. Tolbert was scowling, but when his gaze settled on Angel his frown changed to a smile.

"Ain't you a cutie pie," Tolbert said. "What's your name, sweetheart?"

"Angel." She placed the doctor's bag on the nearby table and unzipped the top compartment. While she did this, Lorenzo circled to the other side of Tolbert's bed.

"You sure look like an angel, yes, you do, indeed." Tolbert smacked his dry lips and rubbed his withered hands together as if sitting down to a meal. "I ain't seen you in here before. I sure would remember if I did."

"We're part of the special care staff," Lorenzo said. "Only our most valuable patients see us."

"Oh, is that right?" Tolbert appeared impressed and confused at the same time. "So, I'm special, eh?"

"Very special." Angel prepared a syringe.

"What you got there, cutie pie?" Tolbert asked.

"Something to help you sleep, sir," Angel said.

"Huh?" Tolbert scratched his head. "I sleep all right. Somebody say I wasn't sleepin'?"

Lorenzo peeled away the bedsheet, revealing Tolbert's emaciated frame.

"Try to remain still," Lorenzo said. "This won't take but a minute, sir."

"Well, all right. Better be nice with the needle or I'll bite ya." He feigned snapping at Angel and cackled.

Angel rubbed the injection spot on his right arm with a cotton swab dabbed with alcohol. She flicked her finger against the hypodermic syringe and gently inserted the needle in his muscle.

The syringe delivered a deadly dosage of potassium chloride. It was one of the three drugs used in many states to execute prisoners on death row via lethal injection. Mr. Tolbert would not expire instantly, but within a few minutes, he would display symptoms of a major heart attack, and that would be the end of his residency at Sunrise Manor.

"You sleep well, sir," Angel said. She kissed Tolbert on the forehead. The old man grinned as if his life's mission were complete, to get kissed by a pretty woman in his final days.

"We're leaving now." Lorenzo shook Tolbert's hand, the man's hand like a dead fish in Lorenzo's grip. "It was a pleasure meeting you, Mr. Tolbert."

Mr. Tolbert's eyes clouded as the poison spread throughout his system. A thin trickle of drool slipped from the corner of his lips.

Angel switched off the lights. They left the television on.

Lorenzo checked his stopwatch app when he started the Navigator's engine. The entire episode had unfolded over exactly fourteen minutes, keeping them well within the twenty-minute window they had available.

He sent his cousin working at the front desk a text message. "All done. God bless."

"God bless," his cousin replied.

As they drove away, Lorenzo resumed his playlist where he had left off. One of his all-time favorites kicked off: "Papa was a Rollin' Stone," by the Temptations.

He knew all the lyrics, and sang along. He'd first heard the song as a much younger child, and he had loved it from the start, maybe because it resonated with him. He didn't know his father. Mama admitted the man was worthless and she had cut him out of their lives when Lorenzo was a baby, and she said she heard through the grapevine that he had died broke and in debt at a cheap roadside motel somewhere in

Mississippi. She refused to speak his name because she said calling the names of evil people could invoke their unclean energy and poison your life.

Mama was wise in ways he would never be.

He glanced at cousin Angel. "Ready for a trivia question?"

Angel rolled her eyes.

"What Motown act *originally* recorded this song?" he asked. "The Temptations made it famous when they released their version, but they weren't the first group at Hitsville USA to record it. Who was the first?"

"You know I don't know the answer to that, cousin." She flicked her index finger across her phone's screen; Lorenzo caught a glimpse of a dancing cat. "Why don't you just tell me?"

"The Undisputed Truth recorded it in 1972." He chuckled.

But Angel's attention already was focused on her funny feline vids. She lacked appreciation for the finer details of soul music history. Most people did. She was his cousin and he loved her dearly, but she wasn't as special as he was, didn't have an exciting future shimmering on the horizon like he did.

One day, her whole world was going to be in his hands.

13

Saturday evening, Eric had called Mark Deacon. Deacon provided security for the church they attended, but his business offered a range of other investigative services, including finding missing persons. Deacon was scheduled to visit their house that Sunday afternoon for a consultation.

"Do you think I'm doing the right thing?" Eric asked Alyssa as they tidied the family room to prepare for the upcoming meeting. "Am I overreacting?"

"It's concerning that there's been no word from Destiny, still." Alyssa used a long-handled lighter to ignite the wick of a scented candle standing on the coffee table. The soothing fragrance of lavender reached Eric's nostrils. Alyssa continued: "She wasn't at Clive's house, and his behavior is odd as well based on what you've learned."

"Then you agree with me about hiring Deacon to help find her."

"I'd like to say no." Alyssa put her hands on her waist and gave him a direct look. "I'd love nothing more than for Destiny to call you out of the blue and say, what the heck, dad, I'm fine, stop bugging me." Alyssa shrugged. "But I'm not convinced anymore that's going to happen."

After church, they had dropped off their children with Alyssa's younger sister. Her sister had a son the same age as Elijah, and Eric had decided that allowing the cousins to spend time together was preferable to his kids eavesdropping on the meeting with Deacon. It was bad enough that his children had overheard the fight with Clive a few days ago. He wanted to shield them from this ongoing drama as much as possible.

He was still struggling, on his own, to accept the reality of what was happening. Was Destiny okay and just ignoring him? Had something terrible happened to her? Why had Clive gone to Grisby, of all places? Was Destiny with him?

He could not simply sit still and hope everything worked out for the best. Life had taught him that sometimes, things didn't just "work out" because you wanted them to—sometimes, you had to take decisive action. He worried that he was overreacting by hiring a private investigator, but with so many unanswered questions, he decided he could live with the consequences of his choice.

At exactly three o'clock, the doorbell chimed. Eric hurried to answer. He found both Deacon and his sister, Val, waiting outside.

Alyssa had thought it was a good idea to invite Val, too. After all, Val had helped Eric connect with Destiny in the first place. Val was equally concerned about what was going on.

"We pulled into the driveway at the same time," Val said. She winked at Deacon. "Buzz, why you didn't tell me that you were friends with a *GQ* cover model?"

Deacon chuckled in that self-deprecating way of his. He wore khakis and a button-down olive shirt that showcased his muscular arms. A series of tattoos were braided along his forearms and biceps, likely acquired during his service as a Marine.

Eric noticed that Deacon also had a holstered gun attached to his waistband, and Eric figured he had a concealed carry permit. Until then, Clive had been the only other visitor to Eric's house who carried a firearm. Eric found Deacon's armed-and-ready demeanor comforting. He wanted Deacon to take this matter seriously, not indulge Eric like someone who needed to be talked down from a ledge.

Deacon also carried a black attaché case. He shook Eric's hand firmly and greeted Alyssa warmly.

"Let's get to it, family," Deacon said.

They settled in the family room, in matching armchairs gathered in a rough circle. Eric had filled in Deacon yesterday evening on everything he knew, but Deacon had insisted on this formal conference before he started working the case.

If Deacon had been shocked to discover that Eric had fathered a daughter who was already an adult, he didn't let on. Eric got the sense that the guy had seen and done things far outside of Eric's experience and he was impervious to being taken by surprise.

"I'd like to record this discussion, if I may." From his case, Deacon produced a handheld digital recorder about the size of a deck of cards. He placed it on the coffee table in the middle of their circle. "Do I have your permission?"

Everyone uttered their agreement.

"Now, I've worked my share of missing persons cases over the years," Deacon said. He took an iPad out of his case, along with a sheaf of papers held together with a paper clip. He distributed the papers to them. "I've located teenage runaways, deadbeat dads, you name it, I've tracked them and found them. A certain set of rules always applies. Please check out the list of Do's and Don'ts I've passed around."

Eric scanned the list of tips. It was mostly common-sense advice. Talk to the subject's friends; don't touch their computer since it may contain clues for an investigator to review; file a missing persons report with the local police department, and so on.

"Before we get into this," Val said, "can we think about whether Destiny has actually run away? It seems she's probably hooked up with her boyfriend and doesn't want to be bothered with us."

"I thought about that," Eric said. "According to Clive's son, he went to Grisby. He didn't know if Destiny was with him or not. Probably she is. But why isn't she communicating with any of us? And why is Clive in Grisby? No one goes to Grisby unless you have a good reason."

"We've got a number of possibilities." Alyssa sipped from her mug of mint tea. "I think that's where Mr. Deacon here can probably assist."

"We can't assume anything at this stage." Deacon tapped his iPad; the scar on his cheek dimpled as his jaws tightened. "But we need to keep in mind, people, this young lady, at twenty-years-old, is an *adult*. Perhaps just barely, but legally she's at the age of majority. Since she's not a teenager, there are limits to how much legal machinery we can put to work on our behalf."

"That's why I didn't call the police," Eric said. "She's grown. I don't have any real proof that her life is in danger and I'm not calling the cops without evidence. They'd laugh at me."

"You can file a missing person report," Deacon said. "I strongly suggest you do so, for the record. But don't expect miracles. I'll walk you through all of the steps and what you'll need to provide to law enforcement."

"Part of your hefty fee, huh?" Eric asked.

"We won't leave any stone unturned," Deacon said. "That's my motto in investigations like this one."

"No stone unturned." Eric weighed the phrase in his mind. "I'm down with that. We'll do whatever it takes."

"We need to review Destiny's motives," Deacon said. "Someone who voluntarily disappears always has a *reason* for doing so. Exactly what occurred prior to her vanishing?"

Alyssa glanced at Eric. Reluctantly, Eric recounted Destiny's argument with Clive, and his awkward intervention that nearly boiled over into violence.

"She didn't leave behind a note, a message of any kind?" Deacon asked.

"Nothing," Eric said, and Alyssa nodded.

"Before we conclude our meeting, I'd like to check out her living area in your basement," Deacon said. "Possibly I can spot a clue you missed."

"I didn't miss anything," Eric said. "But you're welcome to look."

"It's fair to say that this young lady was torn between wanting to stay with your family, and her loyalty to her boyfriend," Deacon said.

"I was a little too heavy handed, I guess."

"I would have done the same thing, brother," Deacon said. "Don't beat yourself up over trying to protect your daughter. But like I said, she's an adult."

"An adult making bad decisions," Eric said, and Alyssa and Val cut their eyes at him. "Sorry, but it's the truth. She needs to leave that loser."

"What I want to explore, in more depth, is Destiny's family background." Deacon balanced a stylus above the iPad's screen. "What do we know about this young lady's life, before you discovered she was your child?"

Eric told him what he knew, which was only what Destiny had shared with him: Destiny had been raised in the foster care system for the first half of her life, revolving through several homes in the Atlanta area. When she was ten, a husband and wife in Atlanta formally adopted her and she enjoyed a time of relative stability. But when the parents divorced, the father moved out, and chaos reentered her life; six months ago, her adoptive mother died of breast cancer. By then, Destiny was living on her own and hooked up with Clive.

"Got it, got it," Deacon said. "Did she mention having siblings from her adoptive family, maybe aunts, uncles?"

"She told me about a couple of brothers," Val said. "They were adopted, like she was. But I don't know their names."

"I know the name of the adoptive mother, for what it's worth," Eric said. "I'll provide that information to you. I don't see how any of this will matter, though. She's deceased."

"I like to be thorough." Deacon's eyes were sharp. He shifted to face Val. "And after her adoptive mother's death, she connects with you on *Ancestry.*"

"I knew right away that she was Eric's girl." Val smiled at Eric. "She's a spitting image of him. He couldn't deny her if he tried."

"I've seen the photo," Deacon said. "I want to know about the maternal side for this young lady. What can you tell me?" His gaze drilled Eric.

"Not much." Eric felt beads of cold sweat gathering on his forehead. "I don't remember her mother."

"Oh?" Deacon's eyebrows arched. "You don't seem like the type, Newton."

"What type?" Eric asked, probably more sharply than he needed to ask.

"I've attended church with you for eight years. We've participated in the men's ministry. You don't seem like the type of brother who would father a child, even when you were in your twenties, and have no idea who the mother could be. I'm an astute judge of character and it doesn't fit."

"I didn't think I was the so-called *type* either until a month ago." Eric dragged his hand down his face. "Do you think I'm proud of that?"

"Eric had an accident many years ago, shortly before Destiny was conceived," Alyssa said. "He was in a coma for two weeks. Did he tell you about that, Mr. Deacon?"

"Do tell." Deacon leaned forward in the chair.

"There isn't much to tell." Eric shrugged. "I was out driving one night—in Grisby—and a deer crossed the road and I swerved to avoid hitting it. I don't remember anything after that, but apparently, I had a head-on collision with a tree. Hit my head, blacked out. Someone driving past saw the truck and called an ambulance. I was in the hospital for two weeks, in a coma."

"Two weeks in a comatose state?" Deacon whistled. "Brother, you are fortunate to have survived. Quite blessed. Did you have any permanent brain damage, spotty recollection of events?"

"I checked out with a clean bill of health."

"But you have no memory of Destiny's mother," Deacon said.

"Listen, my wife is a licensed counselor, she's got a PhD in psychology. If I had memory problems, I think she would have noticed by now."

"Why don't we discuss Destiny's records on *Ancestry*?" Alyssa said. "Babe, show him what Destiny gave you."

Eric opened the manilla folder on his lap. It was a screen print from Destiny's DNA matches on *Ancestry.com*. She had given it to him a couple of weeks ago, fishing for information about her mother.

The family tree broke out matches in order of closeness of relation. In the "Close Family" and "1st or 2nd cousin" sections, there were names that Eric recognized: his sister Val's for one, and a few other members of their family, on their mother's side, who had *Ancestry* profiles.

There was also a name in the cousin section that Eric didn't recognize: Maurice Turner. Val didn't know the name, and the person wasn't linked to her profile. That meant this individual wasn't connected to Eric's family. Maurice Turner was on the side of Destiny's mother, whoever that was.

Eric passed the sheet of paper to Deacon. Deacon scrutinized the data, brow furrowed.

"Maurice Turner is the mystery name." Alyssa glanced at Eric. "I think your girlfriend from the period of your accident would be worth contacting again. Put that name Maurice Turner in front of her and see what she says."

"She already told me she didn't have a child by me—or anyone," Eric said.

"Heaven forbid she could be lying," Alyssa said. "She could have given birth to Destiny and immediately put her up for adoption. Not everyone wants the responsibility of raising a child."

"She makes a valid point," Deacon said. "I'd like you to follow up on that, Newton."

"Pointless." Eric shook his head. "We need to focus on Grisby. Why is Clive there? We find Clive, we find my daughter."

"We'll loop back to that angle." Deacon gave a dismissive wave. "I need to fill in more background data. Let's talk about Destiny's friends, hangouts, et cetera."

Alyssa, Eric, and Val shared what they knew—which wasn't much —about Destiny's hangouts and friendships. Deacon wanted to know if Val's daughter, Jalen, might have some insight, perhaps a closer connection to her newfound cousin. Val looked doubtful but promised to ask her.

"Now back to the real leads," Eric said. He sent Deacon a text message with a photo attached. "That's a picture of Clive's license plate. I snapped it yesterday when I went to his house."

"I've got contacts who can run this plate." Deacon nodded. "We can find out if he's got any priors."

"Can you ping Destiny's cell phone while you're at it?" Eric asked. "I know that's possible. What's involved there?"

"Whoa—are you trying to do my job for me, brother?" Deacon chuckled. "Technically, I don't have access to ping a phone, but I've got connections who might be able to assist. We're not going to miss any steps. No stone unturned, like I said."

"Pinging her cell phone seems like the most straightforward approach," Alyssa said. Val murmured in agreement. "How long would it take for you to do that?"

"These things take time, folks." Deacon used his stylus to swipe and tap the tablet screen. "I'll provide daily updates for the first week."

"How long do you think it'll take you to find her?" Eric asked.

"Most young people who run away don't plan far ahead," Deacon said. "They're acting impulsively, and don't bother to effectively cover their tracks. I expect we'll get resolution soon."

"Within a week?" Eric asked.

"Ninety-eight percent of similar cases are closed within nine days." Deacon pointed at Eric with his stylus. "But I've got work for you to do, too."

"I'm going to Grisby," Eric said. "Not sure if you want me to or not, but I'm going. I know people there. I can ask around about Clive. It's a small town, people talk."

"An outsider would stick out," Val said.

"Before you rush off to play amateur sleuth, there are some other steps you ought to finish," Deacon said.

"I'm all ears," Eric said. "Whatever it takes to get to the bottom of things."

"Print out some missing person flyers," Deacon said. He handed Eric another sheet of paper that had a grayed-out photo and the word "Missing" on top in bold letters. "This is a template for you to follow. I'll also email it to you. Paste in a good, color photo of your daughter's face and some details about her appearance—height, weight, notable physical markers such as tattoos—and provide a phone number for people to call with information. Offer a reasonable reward if you can."

"We can definitely offer a reward," Eric said, and Alyssa nodded in agreement.

"Also, I suggest using a burner phone on the flyer," Deacon said. "You don't want a bunch of crackpots getting your regular phone number and cluttering your voice mail with false leads. When money is offered you can open the floodgates to the loonies."

"Burner phone, got it." Eric bobbed his head. "I can work on this flyer today, then head over to the FedEx shop and make a hundred copies or so."

"Hand them out when you go sleuthing in your hometown," Deacon said. "If you insist on doing that."

"I insist—I'm driving to Grisby tomorrow morning." Eric looked at Val. "You heard that, sis. I'm taking the day off from work. This is my top priority."

"Do what you gotta do, Buzz," Val said. "I've got your back."

"So do I," Alyssa said. She reached out and grasped Eric's hand. "I'll think about what I can do to help, too. We're all in this together."

14

The next day, Monday, Eric started driving to Grisby at ten o'clock in the morning, after rush hour had ended. Without traffic the drive took about ninety minutes; there was no point in leaving his house until folks had gotten to work.

He had been hoping, perhaps naively, that he would wake that morning to find a text message or a voice mail from Destiny. *Hey, I'm back! Sorry, my phone was broken and I couldn't reply, I'm staying at a friend's because I needed to get some space . . .* but there was nothing. His text messages to her in the past few days documented an increasingly desperate, one-sided conversation.

From: *Destiny, it's your father here. I'm sorry for what happened last night. I really need to talk to you. Are you there?*

To: *Hi, me again. I haven't heard from you. Are you okay? We're worried. Please text or call. You can talk to Alyssa if that's easier. Here's her number.*

And the latest: *Destiny, please, if you get this, text me or call me back. Please.*

On the passenger seat lay a manilla folder bulging with flyers that he had printed at the local FedEx store the day prior. *Missing: Destiny Chambers* stated the headline. He had found a good color picture of Destiny and pasted it onto the flyer. He did the best he could to recall details of her appearance that could stand out. The battle angel tattoos on her arms were a distinctive marker. He also included her ethnicity (if it wasn't obvious to someone looking at her photo), eye color (light brown, like his own eyes), height (five-four), weight (about one hundred and fifteen pounds), and date of birth in October.

Deacon had suggested purchasing a burner phone and putting that number on the flyer, and Eric had followed his advice. The prepaid phone rested in a compartment in his truck, all charged and ready to go.

I'm going to help, too, Alyssa had said before he left the house. But his wife was coy about the details of what she planned to do, probably because she knew he wouldn't approve. He had a sneaking suspicion that she was going to track down his ex-girlfriend.

Waste of time, he thought.

Traffic flowed smoothly, and on the last leg of his trip, he exited I-75 South and hopped onto Georgia State Highway 155, which would carry him right into Grisby.

He always had mixed feelings about driving on 155, would often feel a raising of hairs along the nape of his neck. On a stretch of that same state highway, he had plunged off the road and into a two-week coma.

He knew the exact location of his accident, but it had changed in the two decades since the incident. A BP gas station had been constructed in the vicinity of where he had collided with the tree. But the exact tree had not been cut down—it was an enormous oak, probably a hundred years old. It stood just past the gas station, on the right side of the road.

It was a bright morning, nothing whatsoever like that rainy night so many years ago. Nevertheless, when Eric passed that tree, he felt a chill come over him as if someone had walked across his grave.

He shuddered. His cell phone chimed. It was Mark Deacon.

Hope soared in Eric's chest. What if Deacon had found Destiny already?

"Do you have a minute, Newton?" Deacon asked.

"One moment." Eric didn't like to get into detailed phone conversations while driving; he had almost died in a car wreck and had been extra cautious ever since. He found an empty lot ahead and swung into it, shifted into Park. "What's the news? Did you find her?"

"Patience, brother." Deacon chuckled softly. "I've got a hit on Clive Johnson's license plate."

"Clive Johnson," Eric repeated the name. "I never knew his surname. We've already made progress."

"From running his plate, I tied him to some databases. He's got a long record. In a nutshell: the brother's a conman. He has a series of offenses: identity theft, credit card skimming, writing bad checks, impersonating a police officer. He's also got two DUIs."

"A real winner," Eric said, a sour taste in his mouth. How the heck had Destiny hooked up with this guy? Did she know all of this about him? If she did and decided to move in with him anyway, he had to seriously question her judgement.

"Can you send me a mugshot of him?" Eric asked.

"He's got a port wine stain birthmark," Deacon said. "Brother stands out for sure. Mugshot file is on the way—I'll text it."

"How about pinging Destiny's cell phone?" Eric asked. "Any luck with that?"

"These things don't move that quickly, Newton. You've got to give me a couple of days, minimum. Remember, that's a gray area."

"Can we expedite it, for an extra fee?"

"It doesn't work like that. I've got contacts who do this sort of thing on my behalf. Paying more money won't move it along any faster because there are guidelines they need to follow on their end. Windows of opportunity if you will."

"Well, I'm in Grisby. I've got contacts here I'll be chatting with today."

"Glad to hear it. It may help. Keep me posted on any updates."

Eric ended the call and opened the text from Deacon. Clive's photo was attached. It looked like a recent mugshot: gray stubble peppered his cheeks. He glared at the camera.

Asshole, Eric thought. *Where is my daughter?*

Eric pulled back onto the road. The state highway carried him to Cowart Road, which cut through the heart of Grisby.

Eric cruised through the downtown business district. Although the character of the area had changed since his youth, mostly for the worse, one notable place from his childhood continued to thrive: the barbeque restaurant on the edge of downtown. Eric smelled the food before he pulled into the parking lot of Pop's BBQ, and it triggered a twinge of nostalgia.

Pop's BBQ operated out of a one-story, painted brick building standing on a broad swath of property. A covered patio featured plenty of benches. Fragrant smoke spouted from ventilation pipes jutting out of the roof.

At eleven-thirty, the enormous parking lot was about half-full. Good. He ought to be able to grab a few minutes of the owner's time.

He swung into a spot near the front door and headed inside.

15

Pop's BBQ had been a Grisby institution for three generations. Originally owned by his friend's grandfather, then passed down to his father, and eventually, to him, the place did a thriving takeout business and had remodeled their dining room a few years ago to accommodate more dine-in customers. A long, polished bar dominated one wall; wooden tables were located throughout the rest of the cavernous space, covered with the classic red-and-white checkered tablecloth.

Classic R&B played on the sound system: a song by The O'Jays, "Living for the Weekend." Autographed photos of celebrities hung on the wood-paneled walls, too, people who had visited in the course of the restaurant's long history: Danny Glover; Evander Holyfield; Whitney Houston; Whoopi Goldberg; and many others.

Eric didn't see his friend when he entered. He told the host he'd grab a seat at the bar. He made his way across the room and settled onto the leather stool.

The bartender on duty was a fifty-something woman with smooth ebony skin and a neatly kept Afro flecked with gray. Her name tag read Angie. She slid a laminated menu toward him, but Eric didn't need to see it: he had been ordering the same meal at this place for over two decades.

"A large sweet tea, please," he said. "And the half rack of spareribs with Cajun fries and collards."

"You order like a regular." She smiled, flashing a gold tooth.

"Born and raised on it." He smiled back. "Is Smokey here? Tell him his friend Eric Newton wants to chat."

"I'll let him know." She didn't yell for Smokey to come up front. She picked up a cell phone and tapped in a message. "He says, give him five minutes."

Angie slid a tall glass of sweet tea across the counter. Eric took a long sip and felt a shiver of delight pass through him. He needed to watch his sugar intake these days—diabetes ran rampant on his mother's side of the family—but the occasional treat was worth it.

Within a few minutes, Angie brought his food, on two separate plates. The meat lay on a gigantic platter, the spareribs swimming in the restaurant's secret recipe barbecue sauce, two pieces of white bread flanking the protein. The fries and collard greens were served on the other plate, the greens clustered in a small bowl.

As Eric bowed his head to start eating, a hand fell on his shoulder like a bear's paw.

"Newt!" Smokey shouted. "What's up, old-timer?"

Grinning, Charles "Smokey" Washington rounded the bar counter. He wore a plaid shirt, denim overalls, and a red baseball cap twisted backward on his bald head. Eric had always thought Smokey bore a strong resemblance to Luther Vandross, but as Smokey was quick to admit, he couldn't sing worth a lick.

Eric had last seen Smokey about three months ago, when he and Alyssa had visited after spending time with his grandma at the nursing home. He still found Smokey's transformation surreal. Smokey had battled obesity for much of his life until he decided to get bariatric surgery. After surgery, he shed ninety pounds. The slender version of Smokey still didn't quite mesh with Eric's memories of his friend, but he was happy for him. They weren't kids anymore and had to take their health seriously.

They shook hands across the counter.

"Sort of a surprise, seeing you up in here on a Monday," Smokey said. "Are you pushing real estate in Grisby now, Newt?"

"I'm looking for my daughter," Eric said. "She's twenty, about to turn twenty-one." He wiped his fingers on a napkin, opened the folder he had placed on the counter, and slid the flyer toward Smokey.

"You got a twenty-year-old daughter, man?" Smokey frowned. "Since when?"

"Since a month ago. Long story." Eric tapped the photo. "Have you seen her?"

Smokey slid on the pair of reading glasses that dangled from a cord around his neck. He picked up the flyer and examined it.

"Damn, she looks a helluva lot like you," Smokey said. "Cuter, though, if you don't mind me saying. But I haven't seen her. Is she from town?"

"No, but she could be around. I'm out here looking, figured you might know something since so many people come through here."

"Aw, I'm sorry to hear this, man. Kids these days, huh? Hell, sometimes I *wish* my son would get out the damned house and never come back." Smokey shook his head. "Why'd she run off?"

"Her boyfriend's involved, I think." Eric pulled up the photo of Clive on his iPhone and turned it around so Smokey could see. "Have you seen this guy? He's not from here, either, but I heard he's in town."

"Don't think so." Smokey pursed his lips. "I'd recognize him. He's got that thing on his face, the birthmark." Smokey gestured toward his own face. "Shit, he looks a helluva lot older than your girl."

"Tell me about it." Eric smiled sourly. "Look, this guy's trouble. He's into all sorts of scams—identity theft, card skimming, you name it. He's supposedly down here on business and I think it's got to be related to the shady stuff he's involved in. Do you have any idea who would run in those circles here in town?"

"Hmph." Smokey stroked his finely tapered beard. "Funny you ask, Newt. Two months ago, I had to fire a young lady 'cause she was skimming credit cards on the sly. Pissed me the hell off. I can't have folks who work for me stealing from my customers. It would ruin my reputation."

"What's her name?" Eric asked.

"Let me check in my office." Smokey picked up the flyer again. "Hey, can I pin this up in here? You're handing these out?"

"Please do."

While Smokey wandered away, Eric checked his cell phone again. Looking at his phone had become an even worse habit than usual. But there were no messages, from anyone. He returned to his meal, but was no longer as hungry as he thought he was. These days, talking about Destiny tended to spoil his appetite.

Smokey returned about five minutes later. He slid an index card across the counter. It had a name and an address scribbled on it.

"Laronda Moore," Eric said. "Over on Calhoun and Eighth Street? I remember, it's a little rough over there."

"Ain't nothing changed," Smokey said. "Tell her I sent you, too. I could have pressed charges on her black ass, but I settled for firing her. She owes me."

"I'll chat her up. If she moves in those circles, maybe she knows something about what Clive is doing here."

"You be careful, Newt," Smokey said. "Things are changing in town, here. It's not the sleepy little town we grew up in, not anymore."

16

While on his way to visit Laronda Moore, a funeral procession disrupted traffic. A police officer riding a motorcycle led the long stream of vehicles, headlights glowing as they drove along the boulevard.

It summoned a poignant memory for Eric. The day of his grandfather's funeral, hadn't they driven this same somber path from the funeral home to the cemetery? Eric, Val, and Grandma Nellie had sat together in the limousine (Eric's first time riding in a limo, ever), Eric staring out the windows as gathering traffic waited for their procession to pass, people in their cars likely wondering who had died, and how.

He shook his head as if clearing away dust. The vehicles passed, and he resumed his journey.

Laronda Moore lived on the seedy side of town, which for Eric's entire life had been known as an area rough around the edges. He knew he had arrived there when the quality of the road abruptly declined from smooth pavement into a cracked, pothole-riddled mess.

He saw old, dilapidated homes built in the sixties and earlier, many of them with boarded-up windows and rusting vehicles parked on weed-choked lawns. An ancient-looking stove stood in someone's front yard; a ratty sofa with missing cushions sagged near the front steps of another house. Although it was just past lunch time, he saw a good number of people wandering aimlessly around the road, mostly young men who scrutinized him as he cruised past in his luxury SUV.

Eric felt a band of tension tightening across his stomach. He didn't expect anyone to confront him over his presence in the area, but he needed to be about his business and then move on.

The address Smokey had given him belonged to a green ranch-style house that stood on a small lot of threadbare lawn. He spotted baskets of colorful flowers hanging on the porch, and the house looked as if it had been recently painted. Whoever lived here cared about their property.

He parked in front of the house and strode to the front door. The screen door was closed, but the door beyond was open. Eric knocked, the screen rattling underneath his knuckles.

"Yeah?" A brown-skinned young man of perhaps eighteen or nineteen opened the door. He wore a sleeveless white t-shirt with a crimson Kool-Aid stain on the chest like a gunshot wound, and jeans that hung low on his hips, exposing plaid boxers. He yawned as if he had awakened from a nap. "You here for my sister?"

"If your sister is Laronda Moore, yes," Eric said. "Is she here?"

"She at work." He yawned again, scratched his head. "She at the hotel."

He seemed quite comfortable sharing this information with a stranger. Eric wondered about this kid's experience welcoming people to the house to meet his sister.

"Which hotel?" Eric asked.

"Sunshine or something."

"Is there someone else here who might know for sure?"

"My grandma sleep and she'll get mad if I wake her up." He yawned again. "I ain't waking her up."

"The Sunshine Inn, you say?" Eric had never heard of such a hotel in town, but it wasn't as though he had been searching for one. "Is that in Grisby?"

"I guess so."

"Thanks, son." Eric turned away.

Maybe he would come back another time. He didn't know what the boy was talking about.

But it was ironic that Laronda Moore had found employment at a hotel. Someone accused of card skimming working in a business where she would have ready access to an abundance of cards was just too rich.

As he climbed into his SUV, Alyssa called him. He took the call over the vehicle's Bluetooth connection.

"Any news?" she asked.

Eric filled her in on what he'd learned from Deacon about Clive, and his visit with Smokey.

"I've got to find this hotel next," Eric said.

"Please be careful," Alyssa said. "If you start digging your nose where it isn't wanted—"

"I'm not going to walk into anything stupid. Anyway, what are you doing?"

"I'll fill you in later," she said, and that was when Eric knew she was up to something. "Call me when you're on your way back home."

After ending the call, Eric searched on *Google* for hotels in Grisby. There were six of them, all but one located along State Highway 41, which ran North-South along the western edge of town. He scrolled down the list of names. They were all of them chains: Comfort Inn, Quality Inn, Red Roof Inn, Days Inn.

He could be at this all day. Instead of sitting stationary in the vehicle, he decided to drive to the area and start looking, and hoped that something would strike him that would match what the kid had said.

State Highway 41 was a busy stretch of road, studded with chain restaurants, big box stores, and the hotels. The businesses were in an unincorporated region of Spalding County, and about the only section of town that had seen any recent economic development. Eric kept to the right-hand lane and crawled along as slowly as he could. He studied hotel signs when he saw them.

There was no such place as the Sunshine Inn. He had already verified that via Google but hoped that a first-hand view might prove otherwise.

But as he neared the sign for the Days Inn, the design of the logo sparked an idea: a glowing sun, in the background. He swung onto the adjacent road and veered into the hotel parking lot.

If he were wrong and this wasn't where Laronda Moore worked, he decided he would call every hotel on the list and ask for her. No stone unturned, as Deacon had promised.

He went inside the lobby. A petite woman wearing blue, cat-eye style glasses stood behind the front desk. Her name tag read "Viola."

"I'm looking for Laronda Moore," Eric said, before she could ask him if he needed to book a room. "Does she work here?"

"Laronda's on break," Viola said. She rolled her eyes.

Score one for the home team, Eric thought. "Well, I'll wait for her."

"You can probably find her outside smoking." Viola frowned to indicate her disapproval of the practice.

Eric left the lobby and returned to the parking lot. He noticed, at the edge of the lot, a young woman leaning against a green Toyota Camry parked in the shade of a droopy crepe myrtle. She wore a hotel uniform. She smoked and talked animatedly on a phone, her back facing him.

Eric approached. "Laronda Moore?"

She spun with an accusatory glare, as if ready to cuss out a co-worker over interrupting her break. Her expression was tight as a knot. She had long hair dyed red, a tattoo on the side of her neck, and more decorative ink along both arms.

"Who's askin'?" she said.

"I'm Eric Newton. I'm a good friend of Smokey's, from Pop's BBQ. Can I please talk to you for a few minutes?"

"Smokey, huh?" She gave a sour expression, as if his name was like a sip of spoiled milk. "You a cop?" Blowing out a plume of smoke, she gave him a quick once over. "Nah, you ain't no cop. You too soft."

He let the insult slide. "I only want to ask a few questions and I'll be on my way." He lifted one of the missing person flyers. "I'm looking for my daughter. You might know something that can help me find her. Please."

Her gaze didn't register any recognition, but Laronda told the person on the phone she'd call them back. She flicked her cigarette to the ground and stubbed it out with her sneaker.

"I gotta be back at the front desk in like eight minutes," she said. "Make it quick."

17

After tossing her cigarette, Laronda Moore packed two sticks of spearmint-flavored gum into her mouth. She smacked on the gum as she stood next to her car and studied the flyer Eric had given her.

"Workin' up in here, I see a lot of people." Laronda nodded toward the hotel. "But I ain't seen her, sorry." She started to give the flyer back to Eric.

"Keep it, please, just in case," Eric said.

Shrugging, Laronda folded the paper and tucked it into a small handbag. "All right, then. Nice meetin' you, mister."

"Wait," Eric said. "So listen, Smokey told me why he fired you."

Her face darkened as if a thundercloud had taken up residence on her countenance.

"I got a good thing goin' on here," she said. "I ain't doin' none of that shit no more. And you said you ain't a cop anyway, so why the hell do you care?"

"Who's running credit card scams in Grisby?" Eric asked. "I don't care about what you did. I need to know who's in that circle now."

"What's that gotta do with your kid?" Laronda popped gum in his face. "You don't make no damn sense."

Eric pulled up the digital mugshot of Clive and showed it to Laronda.

"Have you seen him before?" Eric asked. "He's my daughter's boyfriend. He's here in Grisby. He moves in those shady circles, whatever you want to call them."

Laronda squinted at the photo. "Hmph. I'd say I didn't remember him, but . . ." She tapped the screen with a lacquered fingernail. "He had that red spot on his face and now I do. I seen him."

Eric's heart clutched. "When?"

"Checked in here maybe a week ago?" Laronda squinted. "Yeah. 'Bout a week ago."

"I heard he came here last Friday. Was it before that?"

"Oh, yeah." She popped her gum.

"Then he's made at least two trips here."

"I only saw him a week ago. He stayed here. Shit, he was flirtin' with me."

"Of course he was," Eric muttered.

"Excuse me?" Laronda's eyebrows arched. "Men flirt with me *all the time*." She looked him up and down as if taking the measure of him. "Yup, men like you, too, even though you tryin' to act all professional and whatever. Y'all all wanna piece of this fineness."

"That wasn't what I meant, sorry." Eric pinched the bridge of his nose. "Did he say anything that stands out? Do you know who he might have been here to meet—if he's into scams?"

"I told you, I ain't into that anymore. I ain't giving you no names, fool!" She cackled as if he were a clown, glanced at her phone. "Hey, your time is up. I gotta get back to work or Viola's gonna snitch on me."

"Wait a minute, please." Eric was desperate, but he didn't have any leverage. She was right—he wasn't a cop. He couldn't force her to share any information. "Can I pay you for a name or two?"

"Hell, no—I ain't no snitch." She strutted away.

He raced to keep up with her. "What room did he stay in?"

"I don't know, man." She gave him an annoyed look. "What difference does it make to you?"

"Can you book me the same room you gave him?"

"All right." She tossed her hair over her shoulder. "Come to the desk in a few minutes. I'll see what I can do."

Ten minutes later, Eric had rented a room for one night on the hotel's second floor. He took the exterior stairs to the upper level and used the keycard to unlock the door.

It was an utterly unremarkable room, exactly what you would expect from a hotel at that price point. A basic place to stay for a short duration.

He had no idea what he was doing there, or what he would do next. He had thought, perhaps in vain, that renting the same room that Clive had stayed in might spark some inspiration.

But he only felt tired. He unbuttoned his shirt, took off his shoes, and sat on the king-size mattress.

Within a few minutes, he had stretched out, lying on his back. A couple of minutes later, he drifted off to sleep.

Maybe being back in Grisby triggered it, but Eric dreamed about his accident. A rainy night. Country music on the radio of his granddad's pickup truck. A massive deer streaking across the road. Eric punching the brakes . . .

When he awoke, the bedroom was immersed in shadows. He had no idea where he was or how he had gotten there, and for a moment, he panicked. He reached out, fumbled for a lamp, clicked it on.

The folder full of flyers lay on the nightstand. It all surged back to him like bile climbing up his throat.

Wouldn't it have been great if losing Destiny had been a dream, too? He thought. He couldn't believe he had tumbled into this situation, searching desperately for a daughter he barely knew.

He had been sacked out for nearly six hours. The duration of his nap wasn't surprising. Since Destiny's disappearance, he had been accumulating a severe sleep deficit and operating in a perpetual state of exhaustion. It had finally caught up with him.

He found a text message on his phone from Alyssa, checking up on him. There were no messages from anyone else.

In the bathroom, he splashed cold water on his face, and started to feel grounded again. He shuffled back into the room.

What am I doing here? What's next? Think, dammit.

He stepped to the window. It provided a view of the busy state highway and a string of restaurants, their neon signs glowing in the twilight gloom.

One bar-and-grill called "Jimmy's Spot," had a big, well-lighted sign advertising five-dollar chicken wings and two-dollar beers.

Eric thought about Clive, and what Deacon had shared of his run-ins with the law. The guy had two DUIs, didn't he?

Eric hadn't brought a change of clothes, so he freshened up as best he could, headed out. Jimmy's Spot was within walking distance of the hotel. Eric crossed the street and went inside.

Inside, he found a bar, tables in the middle, leather booths along the walls. An Atlanta Hawks game played on a few flat screen TVs hanging from the ceiling.

The place was nearly empty on that Monday evening. Eric sidled up to the bar.

The bartender turned. He was a Black man, heavyset, and in his mid-forties, with a mole on his cheek. Eric immediately knew him.

"Brian Houston, right?" Eric said.

"Hey." The bartender's eyebrows lifted. "Hey, Newton, right! We went to high school together. Freshman hoops, yeah? I thought I recognized you, man."

"We were on the B team," Eric said. "That was when I realized my NBA dreams were never going to happen."

Brian chuckled. "But it was fun, right? Good to see you, man."

They shook hands. Brian had a gigantic, fleshy hand and a firm grip.

"What brings you here?" Brian asked. "I haven't seen you around in a minute."

Eric took out his flyer. Although his muse had struck him about Clive, it seemed important to show the flyer to everyone he met.

"Haven't seen her, sorry." Brian wiped the counter with a towel. "And I remember faces, and names. Part of the job. We get a lot of regulars in here and they expect it."

"Do you remember this face?" Eric showed him his phone with the mugshot of Clive on the screen. "He's my daughter's boyfriend. I think he knows where she may be."

"Sure do." Brian tapped his face. "He had that birthmark. Yeah. He was in here last week, I think."

Score another for the home team, Eric thought.

"Was he alone, or meeting someone?" Eric asked.

"Funny you ask that," Brian said. He nodded toward a booth across the dining room. "He was sitting right over there with Maurice Turner."

A shudder passed through Eric. Maurice Turner. He knew that name. He had seen it on Destiny's DNA profile. Turner was listed on her profile as a probable first or second cousin, and had to be on Destiny's maternal side.

"Who is Maurice Turner?" Eric asked.

"He's with the Cannons, man." Brian frowned as if this should have been obvious to Eric. "I mean, he was like ten or twelve years ahead of us, but he's with the Cannons. I think his mama was a Cannon."

Another, deeper chill settled into Eric. The Cannons—the huge family that had a lock on so many businesses in Grisby. Their empire included the nursing home that Eric's own grandmother had been living in for the past six months.

If Maurice Turner was a Cannon, that meant Destiny could be related to the Cannons via her mother. Or Destiny could be linked to Turner's paternal side. Eric knew nothing about any Turners in Grisby.

He didn't know what it all meant. But he decided the Cannon connection was impossible. He had never dated a woman from that family. Ever. Sure, he knew plenty of them. But dated? Been intimate with?

Never.

"You look like you've seen a ghost, man," Brian said. "You all right?"

Eric looked up, wiped his lips.

"I need a drink," he said.

18

While Eric was sleuthing in Grisby, Alyssa was investigating, too. She believed that answers awaited somewhere that he was reluctant to explore: the past.

She began her work in earnest after Eric left the house that Monday morning. Their kids were at school, and she had taken the day off from work—that was a simple call to her assistant asking her to reschedule her appointments.

Her plan was to finish everything she needed to do before the school buses arrived that afternoon. But if things took longer than expected, she'd already asked her mother to be on stand-by to watch over the children at the house.

Alyssa went downstairs into the basement, her sneakers thumping down the steps. She switched on the lights.

It was so quiet down there. Destiny hadn't lived with them for long, but already, Alyssa missed her. They had begun to bond, one woman to another. She saw a glimpse of herself in the young lady: a fierce streak of independence, yet a thirst to be loved by all, especially by a father. Alyssa had a complicated relationship with her own dad that had taken years for her to understand and to make peace with after his untimely death shortly after she'd completed undergrad. Sometimes, despite her background as a psychologist, she still felt like that anxious little girl who would never be quite good enough to earn her daddy's full approval.

Alyssa hoped Destiny was okay, wherever she might be.

Alyssa didn't move toward the bedroom they had designated for Destiny; she went to a door on the opposite side of the basement: the storage area.

The door opened with a soft creak, dust drifting into her nostrils and nearly making her sneeze. Usually, they opened this door only a few times a year, to either add items or remove them. If not for Alyssa's mission, she would not have ventured into this space until it was time to haul out decorations for the holidays.

She turned on the light switch. It was a windowless room, measuring about ten by twelve. Modernist shelving stood along the walls, and a handful of large boxes lay on the cement floor. No loose items lay about. Alyssa had insisted to Eric that if they got a basement and used part of it for storage, they had to resist heaping junk all over the place.

What they had in here, see, was *organized* junk.

Well, it wasn't all junk. There were some items they kept in there that had real value: family pictures they hadn't gotten around to framing and hanging; keepsakes from prior vacations that didn't find their way into the rest of the house; beloved baby toys the kids couldn't bear to part with; old documents that might prove useful someday.

One of the boxes had "Eric's Stuff" written in black marker along the side.

Alyssa doubled back to the main area of the basement, found a chair, and carried it into the storage room. She eased onto it, then peeled open the flaps of the box, dust fluttering away.

She had never looked inside of it and was unprepared for what she would discover. At first glance, she was disappointed.

The box contained a dizzying array of totally unrelated items, and she wondered why Eric had saved these things. A stapler—why would you keep a stapler? A Rolodex that a casual flip through revealed to be empty of names, and who used a Rolodex anymore? A college textbook that Alyssa thought she could probably sell, but it was so outdated it might not bring anything worthwhile on the resale market.

"Junk," Alyssa muttered. As she examined items, she placed them on the floor beside her. She decided that since she was going through the effort of cataloging and rating these things, she was going to throw many of them away.

She found Eric's yearbook from his senior year at Morehouse College; the publication was called "The Torch." She flipped through the glossy pages until she located the photo of him. He wore a black tuxedo like the other graduating seniors, and looked dapper, healthy. But she could clearly see the jagged scar on his forehead that he'd acquired from his car wreck earlier that year.

Underneath the yearbook, she found a bulky Hewlett Packard laptop, the power cord wrapped around it like a dead tentacle. The computer had to be at least twenty years old. An artifact from the time before she and Eric had met.

Alyssa set aside the machine for later examination.

She dug through the rest of the items and found nothing of interest. She gathered the laptop and left the storage room.

In the sitting area section of the basement, she found an electrical outlet next to an end table that held a lamp and a vase of silk flowers. She plugged in the computer and settled onto the sofa with the computer on her lap.

The laptop took ages to boot up and was nearly as loud as a leaf blower. She was worried it would stall on some hard drive issue and never complete the start-up cycle, but after several minutes, she was rewarded with a view of an obsolete Windows desktop.

She guessed this was probably the same computer Eric had used in his final year of college. She could almost understand why he had kept it. She was reluctant to part with old machines, too, worried about data theft and wasn't knowledgeable enough to extract the hard drive and dispose of it properly.

She found the Windows Explorer icon and clicked it.

"Interesting," she said.

There were folders named for various subjects Eric had been taking in college: Accounting Assignments; Finance Assignments; Management Assignments; Math.

There was also a "Photos" folder. She selected it, her heart drumming.

The laptop gurgled and coughed for about a minute, and finally revealed the files contained therein. All of them were .JPEG files, with last modified timestamps of about eighteen years ago, but none of them had descriptive names.

She clicked on each of them. Each file took an eternity to load.

The first one looked like a simple family photo. She recognized the faces: Eric, Val, his grandmother, and his late grandfather, Earl. They were gathered on a patio and smiling for the camera.

A nice picture, and probably it should have been printed and framed. But it told Alyssa nothing useful about the period of Eric's life that most interested her.

She searched all the photo files. All of them were family pictures—some older than others, indicating Eric had been intent to scan old pics—but none of them showed her faces that she didn't already recognize. Mostly, they featured his grandparents, kind souls who had raised him and Val as their own children.

She was searching for pics of old girlfriends, but she didn't see any photos of such women on this computer.

She was about to close the laptop when she noticed the Microsoft Outlook icon. The laptop wasn't connected to the Internet, but wouldn't old email messages be stored on the hard drive?

Like every program on this ancient machine, Outlook took several minutes to open. The program tried to connect to the Internet and flashed an error message. Despite the error, it yielded a treasure trove of old messages.

Her heart rate picked up.

It was at that moment that she truly felt as if she were snooping. As if she was reading Eric's old diary. She looked up from the laptop.

She was alone in the house but imagined how she would feel if Eric were watching her. She could clearly envision his frown of disapproval, his brows furrowing in that distinctive way they did when he was upset.

You don't trust me, do you, babe? When have I ever lied to you?

She reminded herself that she wasn't looking for evidence of past sins. This was for a just cause. She was trying to find his child, and that meant identifying the mother of said child. He said he couldn't remember any prior, meaningful interactions with women outside of his girlfriend at the time, and she believed him.

But: the answer might be stored in these old messages.

She moved on.

The most recent email was from eighteen years ago. It looked like correspondence between Eric and an HR recruiter who had reached out to him to schedule a job interview at a bank.

She scanned every message in the Inbox. The oldest message was dated twenty-one years ago. It was in regard to a school project, an email to the professor about the guidelines.

There were about a hundred and forty emails, total, still residing on the machine; that included sent messages and the received ones. Alyssa scanned the subject lines and recipients.

She found, at last, an email from Rachel Watts.

Rachel Watts was his girlfriend during that period. Apparently, she was a student at Clark Atlanta University because the email domain referenced the school, cau.edu.

Alyssa sat up straighter and read the email.

I get the message, Eric. Why can't you be a man and admit you want to move on? I don't have time for games. I'm worth more than that.

"Uh oh, sounds like a breakup," Alyssa said.

The message was dated in June, twenty-one-years ago. It matched what Eric had already confided to her. He said he dated a woman he referred to as Rachel, and that they had broken up twenty-one years ago. And that she was not the mother of any child of his.

Nevertheless, Alyssa used her phone to snap a photo of the message.

She didn't find any more email correspondence with Rachel, or any other women, besides a couple messages to his sister, Val. If Eric was dating frequently during that period of his life, he wasn't using email as his primary form of communication.

Alyssa shut down the laptop and returned with it to the storage room.

Was there anything else? Had she combed through everything?

She looked through the other items in the room, but the box was the only one that held her husband's personal effects from the relevant period. She began putting things back in place—she decided she wasn't going to throw anything out, after all—when she noticed a bulging yellow envelope. It was mostly wedged beneath the bottom flap of the box that contained Eric's belongings.

She fished it out.

Kodak Picture Processing was printed on the front. It was packed with loose, developed photographs.

The good old days of snapping pictures with cameras and not your phone, Alyssa thought. She opened the top flap.

The envelope contained many of the same pictures that she had already seen stored as .JPEG files on Eric's obsolete laptop. She fanned through them quickly. He must have been scanning them as part of some project to store them indefinitely in electronic format.

Then she saw, near the bottom of the stack, two new photos that weren't archived on the computer.

She eased back onto the chair.

Now this might be something.

19

Alyssa studied the two photographs. Both had timestamps printed on the reverse side, but Alyssa didn't need to see those to know when these pictures had been taken.

One photo showed Eric sitting in a hospital bed wearing a patient's gown, a bandage wrapped around his head like a head band. He looked surprised, as if he had awakened from a long hibernation and didn't recognize his surroundings. Two young, attractive Black women flanked him, the women on opposite sides of the bed: one woman wore navy-blue hospital staff scrubs, her face turned in a rather glum expression; the other woman wore a black sweatshirt with "Clark Atlanta University" inscribed in red letters, and she smiled brightly.

The second picture featured only Eric and the woman with the Clark Atlanta shirt. She sat beside him on the bed, her arm wrapped around him possessively.

Rachel Watts, Alyssa thought. Rachel was there for him when he suffered his accident, and then he dumped her a few months later, evidently. Alyssa felt bad for the young woman. She had been through her share of break-ups and knew how it felt to be committed to someone, only to have them kick sand in your face later.

She studied Rachel's face. Was there a resemblance, however faint, to Destiny? It was tough to discern. But logically, this woman had to be Destiny's mother. The timeline meshed perfectly.

She was going to keep these pictures. She doubted the one including the hospital staff member had any significance—probably it was the same nurse who had monitored Eric during his coma and she was thrilled to see him recover—but perhaps she would show them to Eric later and they would trigger some recollection of . . . something.

She put everything else away and returned upstairs. In her home office on the second floor, she did a *Google* search on a Rachel Watts who had attended Clark Atlanta University. The top result led to a *LinkedIn* profile.

Although twenty-one years had passed, the woman was obviously Eric's old flame. She had changed her hairstyle to a short Afro and her facial features had matured, but there was no denying it was the same woman.

Rachel listed her current employment as "Founder of Cicely's Boutique." Her prior jobs included stints at several major accounting firms, her employment history showing impressive escalations in job titles. It looked as if she had abandoned the corporate world several years ago to start her own business.

Good for you, sister.

Alyssa performed another search and found Cicely's website. The boutique was located in Chattahoochee Hills, in a live-work-play community that Alyssa recognized.

She typed the address into the map app on her iPhone. It was about a twenty-five-minute drive from their home in Roswell.

Alyssa rose from her desk chair.

It was time for a field trip.

20

Cicely's Boutique was based in a wellness community on the edge of Atlanta called Serenbe. Alyssa had visited Serenbe about a year ago to attend a wine tasting with some of her girlfriends. She remembered strolling along the same quaint road that the boutique occupied, the shop wedged between an independent bookstore and an art gallery.

She might have wandered into Rachel's shop during that same visit to browse, might have even seen, in passing, the same woman that she so urgently sought.

It was about one-thirty in the afternoon when Alyssa parked her white Lexus RX in front of the row of shops. In her purse, she had tucked away a few items that she intended to discuss with Rachel.

Eric said he had talked to Rachel recently. Alyssa believed him. She also believed that people lied to protect themselves. A face-to-face chat would give Alyssa a good sense of the woman's integrity; her years of counseling had refined what she liked to call her "truth detector."

She wasn't yet sure how discovering answers about Destiny's mother would lead them to the young lady, but experience had taught her that unearthing the history of a thing often clarified one's comprehension of the present. As the Chinese sage Confucius once said: *Study the past if you would define the future.*

Chimes tinkled when Alyssa crossed the boutique's threshold. It was a warmly lit, inviting space; from visiting the store's website, she already knew the boutique carried an eclectic collection of women's fashion apparel, accessories, and footwear. She might have shopped there if she had retail therapy on her mind.

A salesclerk approached soon after Alyssa entered. She was a cute young woman, her ebony hair styled in two French braids that swished around her shoulders. She might have been the same age as Destiny. If Alyssa were superstitious, she might have interpreted that as a sign.

"Welcome to Cicely's," the girl said. "Is there anything I can help you with today?"

"I love your braids." Alyssa offered a smile. "They look great on you."

"Oh, thank you." The girl twirled one of the strands in her slender fingers. "I'm always changing my hair, but I adore this look. I may keep it for a minute."

"Is Rachel Watts available?" Alyssa asked. A casual glance around the shop hadn't revealed the woman she'd seen in the website photos.

"I'm Nylah, the assistant manager. I can probably help you."

Alyssa saw no purpose in playing coy. "I've got an important, *personal* matter that I need to discuss with Rachel, please. Is she here?"

"She's at lunch. I can tell her you stopped by to see her, Miss . . ." Nylah's tapered eyebrows arched with the unasked question.

"Is she having lunch nearby?" Alyssa nodded toward the street. "I saw a vegan café across the way. Would that be somewhere she frequents?"

"You must have ESP." Nylah laughed. "Honestly, I think she goes there every day."

Actually, when Alyssa had perused Rachel's *LinkedIn* profile, she saw the woman had liked a post about the benefits of the vegan lifestyle. Unintentionally or not, people left digital breadcrumbs that could lead a stranger right to their front door.

She thanked Nylah for her time and crossed the street to the Heavenly Vegan Café. At that time of day, the peak of the lunch hour had passed. Alyssa easily spotted Rachel Watts sitting at a corner booth that overlooked a small pond.

Alyssa approached the table. Rachel looked exactly like her *LinkedIn* photo. She wore hoop earrings and an orange blouse that showed off toned arms. A multicolored headband encircled the base of her short Afro.

Rachel had a tall glass of iced tea and a half-eaten vegan patty in front of her, her attention so riveted on her smartphone that she didn't look up until Alyssa cleared her throat.

"I'm Alyssa Newton." Alyssa gave her best disarming smile. "I'm Eric's wife. I'd like to speak with you for a few minutes if I may. It's important."

"I see." Rachel put down her phone but didn't return the smile. "Eric called me out of the blue a few weeks ago. Lord, talk about a blast from the past." Rachel waved at the other side of the booth. "Have a seat, but I need to get back to my shop soon. I've got a meeting with a new designer I'm hoping to feature."

"I promise, this won't take long." Alyssa settled in front of her. "I visited your boutique. You've got excellent taste. I spotted an Amani X dress that's exactly the sort of outfit I love to wear."

"Is that so?" Rachel's gaze warmed about a hundred degrees. "If you noticed that you've got good taste yourself." She appraised Alyssa with a nod. "It looks like Eric married well. Good for him."

"He filled you in on the adult daughter that's arrived in our lives. She's about to turn twenty-one, this month."

"I already told him I was never pregnant with his child." She seemed annoyed at the very idea, her face tightening. "I was about to graduate, applying to grad school at Emory. Why would I want to have a baby with a man who doesn't want to be with me? I'm worth more than that."

"We're trying to find her." Alyssa took the missing person flyer out of her purse and slid it across the table. "She vanished a few days ago. We're very concerned."

"She looks so much like Eric, my goodness." Rachel studied the photo. "I'm sorry, but I haven't seen her. I can pin this up in my shop if it would help."

"We're trying to cast a wide net, thank you." Alyssa removed the pair of old photographs and slid those toward Rachel, side-by-side. "I found these in Eric's things."

"Wow." A mix of emotions flashed across Rachel's face. She picked up the picture of she and Eric sitting together on the bed. "You know, I thought sticking by him, being there for him through that terrible accident, would mean something." She laughed, a bitter sound. "I was so naïve back then. You've gotta live and learn, as they say."

"Can you identify the woman in the other picture?"

"A nurse, I think." Rachel glanced at the photo. "I remember, she seemed sad to see Eric go. I can understand getting attached to someone you've taken care of for a while."

"One more thing." Alyssa unfolded the printout of Destiny's DNA results from *Ancestry.com*. She had circled the name, "Maurice Turner," the mysterious first or second cousin who wasn't connected to Val and Eric.

"I've no idea who that is, and before you ask, I have an *Ancestry* profile, too." Rachel gave her a direct look. "This guy isn't on there."

"He's not linked to Eric," Alyssa said.

"Then Eric ought to think harder about what he was doing back then. Whoever the mother is sure as hell didn't have the baby by immaculate conception."

A server stopped by and asked if Alyssa wanted to order anything. Alyssa declined. She didn't want to overstay her welcome; Rachel's hackles were up like a cat's ready to pounce.

But Alyssa wasn't quite done yet.

"Do you think Eric ever cheated on you?" Alyssa asked.

Rachel blinked, the question seeming to catch her off guard.

"It never crossed my mind." Rachel paused, her fingers tracing the edges of her glass. "Eric wasn't exactly a ladies' man. He was on the shy side. I remember I asked *him* out the first time. I always go after what I want." Rachel looked at Alyssa. "My daddy taught me to always assert myself. Take life by the horns. Probably the best advice anyone ever gave me."

"But Eric might have had opportunities," Alyssa said, "you couldn't be at his side twenty-four seven."

"You need to be asking your husband these questions, *Mrs. Newton*." Rachel's jaw tightened. "What did he say?"

Alyssa wasn't going to get dragged into a pointless, he-said, she-said debate. "Why did you and Eric break up? Like you pointed out, you were there for him after he recovered from his accident."

"He was different after the accident." Rachel frowned. "Like a different person."

"Different how?"

"He became much more conservative. Stiff." She sipped her iced tea. "But I get it now. If you almost die and you get a second chance at life, you don't want to take risks. You learn to color between the lines."

Alyssa thought this woman would be shocked to learn about Eric's bold actions as of late. Clearly, the young man he had been before his accident had been lurking underneath the surface, needing only the appropriate trigger. In this case, the trigger was an adult child entering his life.

"Is that why your relationship went sour?" Alyssa asked.

"We weren't a good fit anymore. You know, we were only in our early twenties. You're still finding yourself at that age."

Alyssa didn't respond. She let Rachel keep talking, since she seemed to be winding up for a final pitch.

"Now," Rachel said, leaning forward, "have I proven to you that I'm *not* this young lady's birth mother?" She tapped the flyer. "Is that what this little interview is all about? You had to track me down and ask me yourself?"

"I wanted to hear your side of the story with my own ears."

"I don't blame you, girl. Hmph. I'd probably do the same thing if I were you."

"I appreciate your speaking with me," Alyssa said. "I'm only trying to piece together the full picture."

"When I was much younger, I wanted a family, children, the white picket fence fantasy, and I wanted that with Eric." Rachel finished off her iced tea. "It didn't work out. I moved on, dated on and off but never settled down." She shrugged, smiled. "I did the corporate thing for fifteen years, climbed all the way up to VP. I've traveled all over the world. I own a successful store with loyal clients. I've got great friends. I've got my health. I've no regrets. I'm living my best life."

"We should all be so fortunate," Alyssa said. "Thank you for your time."

Back in her car a few minutes later, Alyssa watched Rachel hurry across the road and enter her boutique. The woman must have seen Alyssa get in the vehicle, but she didn't bother looking back.

Rachel Watts was not Destiny's mother. Alyssa was convinced, now. The timeline fit, but there had to be another answer.

21

"We've got a hit on your daughter's phone, Newton," Deacon said.

When Deacon rang him that Monday night, Eric was sitting in an upholstered chair at the Days Inn in Grisby, his iPad propped up on his legs as he searched Facebook. He was still reeling from the discovery that Destiny's boyfriend, Clive, had met up with their mystery man, Maurice Turner at the bar in Grisby. He couldn't wrap his mind around it. If Destiny was a first or second cousin of Turner, then Eric had fathered a child by a relative of Turner's, possibly a Cannon woman.

The problem was that Eric had never been involved, on any intimate level, with a member of the Cannon family. Ever.

The discovery had given him heartburn that couldn't be traced to the beers and hot wings he'd wolfed down back at the bar. Eric figured the DNA matching system on *Ancestry.com* had to be buggy. It had correctly linked Destiny to Val, but on the Turner/Cannon angle, it could not possibly be right.

And why the hell was Clive meeting with Turner, anyway? Eric's bartender friend confided that Turner drove a hearse for the Cannons. Why would a guy who drove a hearse hook up with a convicted conman like Clive? What was the angle? Why had Clive come back to town a few days ago, chauffeured by someone driving a white Lincoln Navigator?

Eric had located Turner's profile on *Facebook* when Deacon called. Eric snapped upright in the chair, his heart feeling as if it had leapfrogged into his throat.

"Where is she?" Eric asked, phone mashed against his cheek.

"You won't believe me when I tell you," Deacon said. "But my contact double-checked it at my insistence."

"She's here in Grisby?" Eric asked.

"It's a triangulation process involving the cellular towers, so it's not an exact location, but it's clear to me—"

"Where is she?" Eric shouted.

"It looks like she's at your house."

22

At home, Alyssa had finished tucking in the children for bed when she answered Eric's phone call. He sounded out of breath, as if he had dashed up a flight of stairs.

Holding the phone to her ear, she left Elijah's bedroom and slipped into the hallway. She had been expecting Eric to check in and had kept her phone on her person in case he rang her, but his frantic tone set her nerves on edge.

"Hey, Deacon pinged her phone," Eric said. "He says she's at the house."

"Whose house?"

"Our house!" Eric's voice crackled through the speaker.

Quickly, she closed Elijah's bedroom door and checked to make sure Brooklyn's door was shut, too.

"Ok, let's take a step back," she said in an even tone. "You know Destiny isn't here in our house. I would know if she were, and I obviously would have shared that information with you."

"Deacon did the triangulation-whatever thing, and the obvious location is our house, he says, she's gotta be there, it's the only place that makes sense."

"Take a few breaths. You sound like you're hyperventilating."

"I'm fine, all right. Can you look around? Please?"

"Hang on a moment." She hurried downstairs to the first floor. The basement door was closed.

"I'll go check down there," she said. "Why don't you call her number? Maybe I can hear the phone ringing or vibrating."

"Good idea." He hung up.

Alyssa's thoughts raced as she descended the staircase. Could Destiny have returned to their house sometime that day? Alyssa hadn't ventured back into the basement since her research mission earlier that morning. If Destiny had kept quiet, it was entirely possible that she could be down there. But why would she have come back and avoided them?

Alyssa flipped on a set of lights. Everything looked the same as it had earlier. There was no evidence of Destiny's presence.

She listened, her head cocked to the side. She heard a faint chiming sound coming from the direction of the bedroom, where the door hung ajar.

She hurried across the area and pushed open the door. The room was dark. She switched on the lamp.

Nothing had been altered since Destiny had vanished: the bed was neatly made, all items sitting in their proper place.

The muffled ring tone came from inside the nightstand. Alyssa snatched open the drawer.

Destiny's iPhone lay inside, an older model protected in a battered, sky-blue case. As it rang from Eric's call, Destiny's identifier for him, "Eric Newton—Dad" flashed on the screen.

Alyssa picked up the phone and called Eric back.

"Her phone is in the basement bedroom. But she's not here, and I don't see any other evidence that she was here today."

Eric made a noise that was difficult for her to identify. Part moan, part muffled curse, and totally unnerving for Alyssa to hear.

"Eric?" Alyssa asked. "Are you all right?"

She heard him exhale, as if he were counting to ten.

"She didn't leave her phone last week," he said slowly. "I looked in there. I searched every drawer in that room. I looked everywhere. So did Deacon when he came over the other day, and you know he wouldn't have missed it."

"Do you think she came back and put it here, then? Perhaps to throw us off her trail?"

"It was our best shot at finding her. Shit!"

"We don't have a security camera over the basement door." Alyssa glanced toward the doorway. "But I'm not sure Destiny is aware of that."

"Did anyone come to the house today?" he asked.

"I was out for part of the day running errands. Mom came here to hang out with the kids when school let out. That's all, though."

"None of it makes any damned sense. Christ, this is like being punched in the stomach. I knew pinging the phone was going to be the game winner."

"I'm sorry," she said. "Maybe you should stay down there overnight. You sound too wrung out to drive home."

"Right, I've still got business to handle here. I need to stay through tomorrow."

"Care to share any details?" she asked.

"Later. I've gotta think on this." He sighed again, and she could picture him dragging his hand down his weary face. "Either Destiny came back to drop off her phone, or someone's helping her, someone who knows we were trying to track her, and who has a key to our house. Who would do that?"

Alyssa had an idea, but she didn't dare to voice her suspicion without any evidence to support it.

Tomorrow morning, however, she would launch another investigation.

23

On Monday night, Lorenzo and Angel were working again.

The Cannon family owned six skilled nursing facilities. That night, they were visiting one of their facilities in Locust Grove, a town northeast of Grisby. Driving his Lincoln Navigator, Lorenzo pulled into the parking lot a few minutes past eleven o'clock and parked at the rear of the building.

They were on the usual tight schedule, needing to do their work within a twenty-minute window.

The patient who had the privilege of their company was a Mr. Ezekiel Price, seventy-nine years old, originally from LaGrange and now a resident of their fine accommodations for the past nine months. Mr. Price and his family had fallen behind in their monthly payments and intel revealed that their getting out of arrears was an unlikely proposition.

Further, Mr. Price's daughter had been obstinate when a member of their staff politely requested permission to take possession of her father's remains upon his eventual death, for the advancement of medical studies.

In the end, the only reasonable course of action was to put the old geezer out of his misery.

"What y'all doing up in here?" Mr. Price asked when Lorenzo and Angel entered his room. His bedside lamp burned, a dog-eared King James Bible resting in his big-knuckled hands. "Y'all ain't part of the regular nursin' staff."

"We've got something to help you sleep, sir," Angel said, in her delicate way. She opened her black medical bag and removed the syringe and vial of poison.

"I sleep fine, thank you." Mr. Price's face wrinkled. "Hmph. I don't like this this one bit. I'm calling my nurse."

He reached for the handheld device that would have summoned the nurse on duty. Although Lorenzo had been informed that the head nurse was on break, and only their family contact was on call, he didn't appreciate this geriatric prick's attitude.

"We're here to assist you." Lorenzo snatched the device out of the man's grasping fingers. "Remain calm and this will be over shortly."

Mr. Price spat at him--a massive, greenish wad of phlegm. It landed on Lorenzo's chest, effectively ruining his uniform.

Lorenzo's first impulse was to cold cock the old fart in the nose. He could have balled his fist and smashed the man's nose like a soft potato. In the past, he might have done it. But Mama had counseled him about harnessing his temper. She said that "cooler heads prevailed" and that if he were to ever lead the family business, he had to use his brain, not his fists, to gain the upper hand and assert his dominance.

So instead of punching Mr. Price, Lorenzo removed a cotton hand towel from the pocket of his scrubs, folded it, and pressed it against the man's mouth.

Mr. Price's eyes bulged. He shouted against the gag, trying to wrest his head away, but Lorenzo's hand on his mouth was like an iron clamp. The old man's arms flailed, striking Lorenzo's chest. Lorenzo doubled the pressure of the gag against his mouth.

"See, I can be nice." Lorenzo grinned at him. "Remember my face when you go to hell, sir."

After about a minute, Mr. Price's eyes fluttered shut. His arms flopped like dead birds to the bed.

Lorenzo checked his pulse. "He's still alive, only resting now."

"Thanks, cousin," Angel said.

She slipped the needle into Mr. Price's arm.

Just another day in the office . . .

"You did a good job back there, cousin," Angel said, when they were back in the Navigator. "You kept your cool. I thought you were going to pulverize that sucker."

Lorenzo smiled at the compliment. Angel was notoriously stingy with praise. Mama, too, would be so proud of his conduct.

To reward himself, he opened his phone and clicked on the first song of a new Spotify playlist that he had created based on a macabre theme: recording artists who had died in airplane crashes. Good ole' Otis Redding started singing, "Try a Little Tenderness."

Predictably, Angel returned to her cat videos.

Three hours later, their shift concluded, and Lorenzo dropped off Angel at her house in Grisby. He headed to the family compound on the other side of town.

As he steered down the long, winding driveway, he noticed that the light in the upper floor window of the mansion was still aglow. Mama was awake. Did she ever sleep?

After Lorenzo parked in the six-car garage and entered the house, he heard Mama summon him from her sanctum upstairs.

"Baby boy?" she said. "Are you home?"

"Coming, Mama." He mounted the steps of the grand, spiral staircase.

The mansion was enormous, with a dozen bedrooms and just as many bathrooms, and lots of places to hang out and chill. Lorenzo never remembered living anywhere else, but Mama often reminded him that there had been a time when their family had not been so prosperous. That time, she liked to point out, was prior to her assuming control of the family's business.

He knocked on the door of Mama's master bedroom, though the door was open.

"Come in," Mama said from the depths of her suite.

Lorenzo found her sitting at her desk, reading by the glow of a candle, a cup of tea at her elbow. She was reading her favorite book in the world: an accounting ledger detailing the finances of their business empire. Her bifocals were perched on the bridge of her nose, giving her an owlish look.

She set down the ledger when Lorenzo approached. "How are you this evening, baby boy?"

"Exhausted but satisfied. We got a lot of work done tonight."

"You know I'm proud of you, don't you? You're making the right steps. Everything is going to be yours someday. You're my chosen one."

That was the goal that pulled Lorenzo forward; it was why he put in the long hours when others slept. Why he did the tasks that no one else wanted to do, or could do. It was his preparation for becoming the next leader of the family.

"Thank you, Mama." Lorenzo tried to stifle a yawn, but Mama only chuckled at him.

"You can go to bed now, baby." She tapped her cheek with a ring-encrusted finger. "Kiss."

He kissed her cheek. Mama smelled of Chanel perfume and mint tea.

Lorenzo retired to his own bedroom, which was located across the hallway from the master suite. He stripped out of his clothes and, nude, did fifty push-ups on the rubber mat next to his bed. Afterward, he took a cold shower and finally, climbed onto the mattress.

He dreamed about leadership. About being the one who was willing to do whatever it took. The one who did the tasks that others would not. Or could not.

The chosen one.

24

Tuesday morning, Alyssa visited Newton Real Estate's headquarters in Roswell's historic district.

The family-owned company worked out of a restored, Craftsman-style residence in the commerce section of the quaint neighborhood. A yoga studio was located next door in a vintage Victorian home; on the other side, a hair salon operated out of a charming cottage.

As Alyssa pulled into the gravel parking lot at the back of the house, she saw Val's Mercedes SUV parked in the shade of a magnolia tree. A Joro spider had erected a gigantic web between the low-hanging branches, the big, yellow-striped arachnid motionless as it waited for prey to tumble into its trap.

Inside, Alyssa saw her niece, Jalen, working at the front desk. She was nineteen and worked part-time at the office while attending classes full-time at Georgia State. It was exactly the path that Eric wanted for Destiny; the problem was that Destiny didn't want it for herself. You couldn't force a round peg into a square hole. In her counseling practice, Alyssa frequently encountered parents who wanted to shoehorn their children into their own dreams, and it rarely worked out to everyone's satisfaction. Destiny would have to discover her own path.

"Hey, Auntie." Jalen looked surprised to see her. "Is everything all right?"

"Good morning, sweetie. Is your mom available?"

"She's in her office."

"Have you talked to Destiny lately?" Alyssa asked.

It was a gotcha-question. Alyssa wanted only to register Jalen's response.

"Umm, no." Jalen glanced down at her smartphone. "Everyone is still looking for her, aren't they?"

"We had an interesting development last night." Alyssa let the comment hang in the air. "Anyway, I'll go chat with your mother now."

Jalen didn't reply, but she looked relieved to see Alyssa turn her attention elsewhere. Alyssa strolled down the main hallway, passed Eric's vacant office, and knocked on the door of the next one.

"Hey, come in, girl," Val said. She was stylishly attired in a green business suit, her face freshly made up. "I'm about to head out. I'm meeting a seller in Buckhead." She clasped her hands together, her eyes shining. "This will be a big one, we hope."

"Did you hear what happened last night?" Alyssa asked.

"No one said anything to me. Did Eric get some news?"

"Mr. Deacon pinged Destiny's phone. As it turns out, the phone was in the bedroom in our basement."

"Was it?" Val asked. "Then, clearly, it must have been there the entire time. Destiny left it behind. She could have known it could be tracked. She's a smart one, that kid."

"She must have been thinking several steps ahead of us. I find that interesting because I'd say she's a bit impulsive, like many young people her age."

"She's had a harder life than many, must have street smarts," Val said. "Girl, I'd love to chat, but I really need to get going. Traffic on 400 South is crazy. Keep me posted, okay?"

Val hustled out of the office. Alyssa used the restroom and returned to the front of the house. Jalen gazed intently at her laptop display.

"I'll be going now," Alyssa said.

"Oh, okay," Jalen said. "Tell Uncle Eric and the kids that I said hi."

"Did you talk to Destiny yesterday?"

Jalen lowered her head, wouldn't meet Alyssa's gaze.

Guilt could be like that, Alyssa knew: literally a weight hanging like an anchor around your neck.

"I'm not supposed to talk about it," Jalen said in a near-whisper, as if afraid her mother would hear even though Val had left the office.

"Your uncle is worried sick, Jalen. This is breaking his heart."

"I'm sorry. I promised I wouldn't tell." She sounded like a little child, not a young woman going on twenty.

"You promised who?" Alyssa asked.

Jalen still wouldn't meet her gaze. "She's scared. I'm scared for her. She's got that crazy boyfriend . . ."

"Do you have another phone number for her?" Alyssa asked. "Give it to me, please."

"I don't know, Auntie."

Alyssa stood in front of the desk, not moving, not taking her gaze away from Jalen. Just calmly waiting for her niece to acquiesce. Most people—certainly, Jalen—wanted to do the right thing and were uncomfortable keeping secrets. Alyssa got people spilling their innermost secrets as a regular part of her job. She could wait out Jalen's reluctance.

"I've got all day," Alyssa said. "I took the day off."

"I shouldn't be doing this, but whatever." Jalen scribbled a number on a Post It note and handed it to Alyssa. "Please don't tell anyone I gave this to you. I don't want to be called the snitch."

"Thank you," Alyssa said, but she would promise no such thing. "You're making the right decision."

Outside, Alyssa immediately called Eric.

25

Eric was parked at the Grisby Chick-Fil-A working through a chicken biscuit and cup of coffee when Alyssa called him with the news. He nearly spat a mouthful of coffee onto the dashboard.

"Jalen happens to have a backup phone number for Destiny," Eric said. "But she doesn't know where she's hiding? Did she say if Destiny's okay?"

"I was fortunate that she shared the phone number," Alyssa said. "If she knows more, she's not telling."

Eric tossed the remaining portion of the biscuit into the take-out bag. He had lost his appetite.

"Does Val know?" he asked.

"I think you'd have to ask your sister yourself. She was rushing out the door when I saw her."

"Do you think she was behind the phone showing up in the basement?" Eric asked. "Val is one of the few people who has a key to our house."

"That sounds like another topic of discussion between you and your sister."

"But what do *you* think? You're the psychologist."

"I'm not a mind reader, babe. I ask questions. People either answer them or they don't. Usually, what they don't reveal is as telling as what they choose to share."

Eric drained the rest of his coffee, suddenly desperate for caffeine, as he expected he had another long day ahead of him. He was going to call Val; he was going to call his niece, Jalen. Someone owed him some answers.

"I've texted the number to you," Alyssa said. "I suggest that you do *not* reach out to her via this new channel. If she's okay and simply doesn't want us to find her, we need to try to understand what's going on."

"What do you think I've been doing down here?" Eric said. "Sightseeing?"

"I think her fear of her boyfriend is still at play," Alyssa said.

"I promise not to call her, okay? But I need to find her."

He heard Alyssa sigh. "What's next on your agenda?"

"I'm going to see Maurice Turner at home. He's in the phone book. He's the only Maurice Turner in town."

"Please keep me posted on developments."

"What exactly have you been doing?" he asked. "You been quiet about your activities, but I know you've been up to something."

"We'll talk soon, and I'll share all the details. Love you."

She ended the call. He loved Alyssa to death, but sometimes her habit of keeping her cards close to her vest drove him nuts.

Eric rang Deacon and pleaded for a new ping—expedited—on the second phone number. Deacon promised to do his best and repeated Alyssa's same warning: don't try to call Destiny on the new line. If his daughter was in hiding, blowing her cover might trigger her to take off again.

Why was she avoiding him? It didn't make any sense. He wasn't the bad guy here. He was only trying to help her.

Eric next called Val, but she didn't pick up; neither did Jalen. Were they stonewalling him?

He pulled out of the restaurant parking lot. Maurice Turner lived in an older section of Grisby, not far from where Eric had grown up with his grandparents. It was likely that he and Eric had passed each other in the neighborhood and had never formally met.

Turner resided in a split-level house that probably had been built in the 1960s. It was mint-green, with black shutters. The front lawn looked freshly mowed. Two satellite dishes bristled from the roof like insect antennae.

The carport housed a twenty-year-old Cadillac DeVille with a rusted bumper and a cinderblock in place of the left rear tire.

Eric pressed the doorbell. He heard high-pitched barking inside the house and small paws scrabbling at the front door. But no one came to answer.

"Mr. Maurice went off to work," Eric heard a brittle woman's voice say, nearby. He turned to see an elderly Black woman. She sat on a plastic chair on the narrow front porch of the ranch home next door.

Eric hadn't noticed her until then. Her hair was wrapped in a pink scarf. She wore a yellow mumu and white house shoes. A wad of chewing tobacco bulged in her right cheek.

Eric knew it was unlikely, but she might have been the same woman who had watched from her front stoop when he was a kid walking back and forth to elementary school, or playing football in the street. One of those wise women who were like neighborhood landmarks, who knew everyone and their business and traded gossip like stock picks.

"Thanks for the information, ma'am," Eric said.

"I saw him pull that big truck out the driveway this morning, uh huh." She pointed toward the street, as if the vehicle were still in sight and Eric could flag it down if he moved quickly.

"What kind of truck?" he asked.

"Some big silver truck, looks brand new. You know Mr. Maurice drives a hearse for the Cannons. He drove my husband up to Beacon Hill, uh huh."

Beacon Hill was the local cemetery. Eric's grandfather was buried there, too. Although cemeteries in town were no longer segregated, it seemed to Eric that Black folks in Grisby still went where they had always gone for their final earthly resting place.

Since he had the woman's attention, he showed her the missing person flyer. She spat a stream of brownish liquid into a tin bowl and shook her head. A peek at Clive's mugshot on Eric's phone brought another head shake.

"I ain't seen them at Mr. Maurice's, neither," she said.

"I'll catch him at work. Have a good day, ma'am."

It was about a ten-minute drive to the Cannon Funeral Home. The sprawling brick campus with white columns out front stood far back from the road, requiring visitors to follow a winding path to reach the vast parking lot.

As Eric got closer, he groaned. There appeared to be a memorial service in progress, based on the large number of vehicles parked outside. He saw a Cadillac hearse idling beneath the porte-cochere at the front entrance.

He should turn around and come back later, he decided, out of respect to the grieving family. He could possibly catch Turner at home later.

With that decision in mind, he drove closer, intending to turn around in the parking lot and head back. The lot was so crowded that Eric found himself seeking space for a U-turn around the side of the building.

That was when he spotted the white Lincoln Navigator parked in the staff lot. A vehicle exactly like the one that had picked up Clive at home several days ago.

Eric swallowed, his throat clicking. Without any conscious thought, as if his body were on auto pilot, he slid his truck into a spot in a far corner of the lot. He checked his phone for messages, found none, and got out.

Although the hearse was parked in front of the funeral home, Eric didn't see Maurice Turner nearby. He decided to go inside.

In the vestibule, mourners dressed mostly in black quietly filed inside the sanctuary. Muted pipe organ notes floated from within. Eric recognized the song as, "Amazing Grace."

He also noticed a large photograph of a smiling woman displayed on an easel beside the doorway. The caption beneath read: *"Martha Davis: 1930 – 2021"*

A chill washed over him. The decedent was the exact same age as Grandma Nellie.

A red velvet rope separated the sanctuary from the commercial section of the funeral home. Eric stepped around the rope and wandered into the showroom.

The showroom contained a wide collection of caskets, vaults, and cremation urns, the items artfully displayed in appropriately somber lighting. A display case standing on a table held copies of a glossy brochure with a smiling couple on the cover. The header above the photo stated:

"Providing Options in Your Time of Need"

Michelle Cannon, the nursing home administrator, had given him a copy of this same brochure, he remembered. He had trashed it without reading it. Curious, he picked up a copy and flipped through the first couple of pages. Cannon Family Donor Services offered *"free cremation in exchange for donating your loved one's body to advance medical studies."*

Well, that sounds like a helluva deal, he thought sourly, and tossed the brochure back onto the table.

He didn't see any employees nearby. He cast a quick look around, approached a doorway on the far side of the room. A sign that stated "Staff Only" hung on the wall.

He entered and found himself in a long corridor with recessed lights, cream-colored walls, and a dark laminate floor. Several doors, all of them closed, branched off the hallway.

At the end of the corridor, a red "Exit" sign glowed above a door. Eric pushed through the door.

He was at the back of the building. A collection of hearses and other vehicles were parked outside.

The Lincoln Navigator was there, too.

His phone in hand, Eric approached the Lincoln. The rear of the vehicle faced him—the driver had backed into the parking slot—giving him a clear view of the rear license tag. It was a Georgia plate, for Spalding County.

Eric snapped a photo of the plate.

"What are you doing, sir?" a man asked.

Startled, Eric fumbled his phone, almost dropped it. The driver's side door of the Lincoln had opened. A young man glowered at him.

As Eric tried to manufacture a believable story, the guy climbed out of the truck. He was about six-feet-two, broad shouldered, with a neck thick as a tree trunk. He was well dressed in a gray two-piece suit and black oxfords. His hair was cropped in a buzz cut with lines so defined they might have been etched with a laser.

A silver name tag pinned to his lapel said, "Lorenzo Cannon – Ambassador."

One of the Cannon kids, Eric thought. *Shit.*

"I'm looking for Maurice Turner," Eric said. "I know he drives a hearse."

"Cousin Maurice is working," Lorenzo said. "What's your business with him?"

"Is he driving the hearse for today's service?" Eric asked.

Lorenzo advanced, his eyes dark as raven wings. "You didn't answer my question, sir. What's your business with Cousin Maurice?"

"I'll go back inside," Eric said.

"If you aren't here for the memorial service, or to purchase funeral arrangements, I'm asking you to leave the premises."

Lorenzo closed the gap between them and came a shade too close to Eric for comfort. Eric took a step backward. A thick vein pulsed in the center of Lorenzo's forehead, and his big hands were clenched into fists. The kid had an air about him that reminded Eric of a bouncer in a nightclub who was a little too eager to toss you out on your ass. He was perhaps in his twenties, stoked on testosterone and bravado, itching for a fight.

"I'm leaving." Eric turned toward the door from which he had exited.

A towering, broad-figured woman had emerged in the doorway. She was immaculately attired in an elegant black dress and pumps, and a strand of pearls hung around her wide neck. She wore heavy make-up, and her black hair was long and lustrous. He pegged her age at mid to late seventies.

"I've got this under control, Mama," Lorenzo said.

He sounded to Eric like an adolescent boy pleading to be taken seriously.

"Hello," she said. She had a husky voice, and her hazel-eyed gaze penetrated Eric. "I know you. You're one of the Newton children."

Eric didn't know where this woman ranked in the Cannon family hierarchy. Like her son, she wore a silver name tag as well: "Mary Cannon – Managing Director." Did that mean she led the whole operation?

"Yes, ma'am, I'm in the Newton family," Eric said. He added: "We've been loyal customers for years."

"Are you here for the service, Mr. Newton?" She lifted her chin.

"I was just leaving," Eric said.

"You better be." Lorenzo glared at him.

Eric felt both mother and son watching him as he circled the building. When he came within view of the front entrance, he saw a dark-skinned man wearing a suit standing next to the hearse. He wore sunglasses and smoked a Black and Mild cigar, tendrils of smoke wreathing his bald head.

Eric was certain it was Maurice Turner. Eric had seen a photo of him on his *Facebook* profile.

He couldn't risk approaching him here, not with the musclebound Cannon kid hot on his tail. Eric returned to his truck on the other side of the parking lot, but he didn't leave. He waited.

He called Val again. His call went to voice mail. He texted her and it took her five minutes to respond, and she said only, *"Busy. Will talk later."*

His sister was still avoiding him. Behaving like a guilty person.

The memorial service concluded about forty-five minutes later. A police escort arrived on motorcycle, and attendants in orange vests directed vehicles out of the parking lot, into the procession that would travel to the cemetery.

The hearse, as expected, was the first vehicle to depart.

Eric hung behind and joined the procession near the end. They traveled to Beacon Hill, normally a ten-minute drive, but the police escort, allowing them to bypass traffic lights, shortened the journey.

Entering the cemetery brought back memories. Eric visited his granddad's grave twice a year: on Father's Day, and on his grandfather's birthday in mid-November. He knew the layout of the graveyard well. Once he passed through the gates, he diverged from the procession and parked near his grandfather's burial plot, under the boughs of a chestnut tree.

He climbed out of his truck. He could spot his granddad's headstone from where he stood. A lump of emotion filled his throat.

Stay focused, he reminded himself. *Eyes on the prize, Eric.*

He swallowed. The sky threatened rain and the wind picked up velocity. He snagged his windbreaker jacket out of his truck, shrugged into it. He slipped on his sunglasses, too. He didn't want to risk running into someone who knew him.

From his vantage point, he had a good view of the burial ceremony for Martha Davis, and most importantly, he could watch the hearse. He saw Turner get out and open the rear cargo door, but Turner didn't assist with transporting the coffin. The pallbearers, five men in dark suits, hefted the casket out of the hearse.

Turner watched with an air of utter boredom. He checked his phone and jingled his hand in his pocket.

Eric made his way closer, keeping to the edge of the paved paths that wound throughout the cemetery.

About fifteen minutes later, as the burial concluded and the crowd dispersed, Turner got back into the hearse. Eric hurried, concerned the guy might drive away. But Turner only lowered the window and started smoking, the pungent aroma of the cigar tickling Eric's nose as he neared. Music filtered from inside the vehicle. It sounded like the Isley Brothers, "Between the Sheets."

Not exactly something you'd want played at your burial, but mostly everyone was gone except for a handful of mourners talking in hushed tones.

Eric rapped on the driver's side window. Turner gave a start and peered at Eric from behind the wheel as if he feared Eric were a cop there to write him a ticket.

"You need something, man?" Turner asked. He either had a lazy drawl or might have been sliding into a drunken stupor. Eric spotted a silver whiskey flask poorly hidden in the juncture of Turner's legs.

"How do you know Clive?" Eric stuck his phone in Turner's face, the mugshot of Clive filling the display.

Turner raised his sunglasses off his nose and squinted. His eyes were bloodshot, the edges yellowed with jaundice. He looked from the phone to Eric.

"Who're you, man?" Turner asked.

"I'm Eric Newton," Eric said. "This man is my daughter's boyfriend. She's gone missing. I know you met him here in town recently. Why?"

"Aw, man, I don't know that cat." Turner laughed, but it was a nervous sound. "You got bad information, brother."

"This is my daughter." Eric whipped out the missing person flyer and shoved it in Turner's face. "You're related to her. We found you linked to her on *Ancestry*."

"Goddamn DNA." Turner made a spitting sound. "Knew I shouldn't have let my woman talk me into that shit! It ain't been nothing but a headache."

"Why did Clive want to talk to you?" Eric asked.

"Man, I ain't . . . damn." Turner hit the button to roll up the window, nearly trapping Eric's hand inside. Eric snatched out his arm as the edge of the window grazed his hand.

Turner fired up the hearse's engine and took a swig from his flask. Eric pounded his fist against the window.

"Hey! I just need to find my daughter!"

Turner gave him the middle finger and hit the gas pedal. Eric stepped back, lest Turner run over his foot.

The hearse roared away across the cemetery. The flyer tumbled across the dry grass.

Cursing to himself, Eric hurried forward and picked up the paper. As he stood, he saw an unwelcome sight: the white Lincoln Navigator cruising toward him, Lorenzo Cannon behind the wheel.

"Shit," Eric said.

He shoved his hands in his pockets and started walking.

Lorenzo pulled alongside him and lowered the window. "I've got some important information for you, Mr. Newton!"

"What is it?" Eric paused in mid-step, his heart thundering.

Lorenzo stopped the truck and climbed out. He came toward Eric, and something about him, perhaps the look in his eyes, set off an alarm in Eric's hind brain. Eric started to spin away.

But he was way too slow for this kid. The young man was built like a wrestler but was fleet of foot.

Lorenzo grabbed his shoulder with one hand, and drove his other hand into Eric's solar plexus, his fist feeling like a sledgehammer as it slammed against Eric.

Pain exploded in Eric's body. Gasping, he fell to the grass.

Stay away from my family, Lorenzo said, and left Eric there squirming on the ground like a crushed bug.

27

It was raining when Eric finally got back on his feet. He wobbled, groaned. His stomach felt as if he had swallowed a hand grenade. Bent over, hands on his knees, he drew shallow, painful breaths.

The wetness on his cheeks might have been either the cold rain, or tears. No one had hit him since the sixth grade, when Big Tim Jackson had sucker punched him allegedly because Eric had stolen his girlfriend.

He ought to file a police report against the kid. He had his license plate, and his name. He could contact the police and press assault charges.

But what good would it serve? And again, these were the Cannons —they wielded a lot of influence in Grisby. Undoubtedly, some high-ranking official on the police force would prove to be a relative of theirs, and he recalled that a former mayor was a Cannon, too.

In the sleeting rain, Eric dragged himself back to his truck. Thoroughly soaked, he let back the seat as far as it would go and closed his eyes, one hand resting on his aching gut.

Rain drummed against the windshield at a soothing cadence. He felt himself drift, his thoughts unraveling like a ball of thread.

Clive . . . Maurice Turner . . . Lorenzo Cannon . . . Destiny . . . how were they all connected? Why had Turner lied? Where was Clive? Where was Destiny? Was he chasing his own tail in this so-called "investigation" of his? He felt no closer to answers now than he did when he started. The only tangible thing he'd picked up was a terrible stomachache that might have him pissing blood for a week.

The chiming of his phone snapped him back to alertness. Wincing, he sat up.

It was Deacon: "I've got a hit on the new phone."

"Where?" Eric's mouth was dry.

"Duluth. A residential area. I can send you the coordinates we've compiled based on the triangulation."

Eric's mind churned. Duluth? It was a northeastern suburb of Atlanta, in Gwinnett Country. What would Destiny be doing there?

"I'm on my way," Eric said. "Do you want to meet me somewhere in the area?"

"I was going to suggest that. I think it would be helpful to have a non-family member there. I've texted you the info."

"Got it," Eric said. "Oh, someone just assaulted me, by the way."

"You've gotta be kidding me, Newton. You? You're a lamb."

"That doesn't sound like a compliment at all." Eric filled him in on the details as he steered out of the cemetery and joined traffic on the adjacent road. "I took a photo of the plate. I'll send it to you, and you can do your DMV thing."

"Let's see how this latest ping works out first, Newton. Can you get there in ninety minutes?"

He would have to brazenly violate the speed limit to travel from Grisby to Duluth in ninety minutes, but Eric didn't hesitate.

"I'll be there."

28

An unsettling suspicion had settled over Eric when, arriving in Duluth two hours later, he pulled into the gas station parking lot and slid into the spot next to Deacon's black Jeep Gladiator.

"You're late," Deacon said, with a pointed glance at his wristwatch. He was an old school watch guy like Eric.

"I drove as fast as I could, but traffic was awful. Listen, I don't really trust this information of yours."

The scar on Deacon's jaw dimpled. "Explain."

Eric told him his concern. Deacon made a dismissive gesture.

"We need to check it out anyway, Newton. Whether you like what it tells us or not."

"I figured you would say that. No stone unturned, right?"

They got into their respective vehicles. Deacon followed Eric since Eric knew this area well. Newton Real Estate had multiple properties listed in Duluth, and one residence fell right within the realm of possibility for the cell phone's triangulated location.

Eric turned onto a residential street lined with two-story homes standing on neatly tended lawns. Just ahead, a "Newton Real Estate" yard sign stood like a flag. Eric pulled into the driveway and Deacon parked on the street in front of the house.

A lockbox hung on the front door. Eric had the head code to open it and retrieve the key. He let himself inside.

His footsteps echoed across the hardwood floors. The rooms were empty, dense with shadows. Although the home was unfurnished, that wouldn't have mattered to someone seeking shelter.

"Newton?" He heard Deacon at the front door.

"Back here." Eric paused at the threshold of the master bedroom on the first floor.

A sleeping bag lay unfurled on the floor, alongside an empty water bottle and a brown paper bag from Chipotle. A prepaid cell phone lay atop the sleeping bag.

"That our phone?" Deacon asked.

Eric called the number that Alyssa had given him. The phone lying on the floor chimed a default ring tone.

Eric picked up the phone. It didn't have any security measures. He checked call history and found, in the short list, a familiar phone number. He hit the button to call it.

A woman answered, speaking in a whisper: "Hey. Is everything ok, girl?"

Eric terminated the call without answering. He turned to Deacon.

"I've got to get back to Roswell," Eric said. "Val and I need to chat."

29

At his company's headquarters, Eric shoved open the door to his sister's office and tossed the prepaid phone onto her desk.

"Start explaining," he said.

Val looked at him as if he were an escaped mental patient. Two people—prospective clients, surely—sat in armchairs that flanked her mahogany desk. The folks turned, eyes bright and curious.

"Excuse me, please." Val recovered with a polite, fake laugh. "My brother and I need to chat for a moment. I'll be right back."

Eric snagged the phone off the desk as Val stormed out of the office. He followed her into a vacant bedroom they had converted into a conference room. He shut the door behind them.

"Have you lost your ever-loving mind, Buzz?" Turning, Val glowered at him, fists bunched on her hips. "I am here conducting business, *our* business. You know our golden rule."

Eric knew what she meant; it was an agreed-upon condition of their partnership. Within the walls of Newton Real Estate, they discussed work, and only work. Their personal lives were off limits. That strict dividing line had worked well for thirteen years.

But as far as Eric was concerned, Val had crossed that line with her recent actions, and everything about their relationship—business *and* personal—was up for debate.

"We found out about this backup phone." Eric wagged the phone as if it were evidence in a trial. "I know *you* left her original phone back at the house in the basement, too. You have a key to our house, and you know what? Our security camera is pretty damned good—I saw the footage on the phone app. I didn't see you go into the basement, but I saw your car parked out front."

Val's nostrils flared, a sure sign that she was getting seriously pissed. He didn't care. He was the only one here with a right to get angry.

"Now this," Eric said. "You hide my daughter at one of our listings? What the hell for? You see how desperate we've been to find her, and you've been conspiring against us all along? Whose side are you on anyway?"

"She was planning to get a restraining order, Buzz." Val said in a taut whisper. "I was walking her through the steps. You know I have experience with that process from my ex."

"She was getting a restraining order against Clive?"

"No—against Big Bird." Val rolled her eyes. "Jesus, Buzz. I was keeping her *safe*."

"*Then why didn't you tell me?*" He was shouting, and the clients in her office probably heard him.

"Why didn't I tell you? Mr. Father Knows Best? You were smothering her."

"Smothering her?" He felt as if he'd been gut punched, and it hurt far worse than when Lorenzo Cannon had nailed him. "She said that?"

"*I can't breathe around him.* Those were her exact words." Val shook her head. "She was hoping things would work out when she moved in with you, but with Clive coming around that night, and you in her face trying to control her life, it was too much for her. She called me, upset, and I stepped in."

But Eric barely heard the rest of what his sister had said after she'd shared Destiny's remark: *I can't breathe around him.* He tossed the phone onto the conference room table, pulled a chair away and collapsed on it, his legs unable to bear his weight anymore.

You're smothering her.

He had wanted only to help her. To be there for her now that he'd finally learned of her existence. He wanted to do everything for her.

After all, he knew how it felt to grow up without a biological father in his life. His dad had cut bait when he and Val were young children. Their grandfather had been there to step in and fill those paternal shoes, but Eric would be lying if he said he had forgiven his father for his abandonment. Eric had vowed, even as a boy, to be a better father to his future children than his dad had ever been to him.

That included Destiny. He had missed twenty years of her life. He was determined to make up for that lost time. He had to be there for her, in every possible way. He had to be the perfectly reliable father that she deserved, the one who rescued her from bad decisions, who smoothed the rough roads of her life.

I can't breathe around him.

How could he have misjudged the situation so badly? This young woman didn't want his help. She didn't appreciate his well-intentioned advice, his hard-won wisdom. Although he could clearly see that her poor decisions would lead her to heartbreak and pain, she wanted him to stand aside, let her fail, let her stumble, let her suffer . . . yet be there, presumably, to pick up the pieces when she finally admitted that she needed him.

He couldn't understand it. He cradled his head in his hands.

"Now, she's gone," Val said. "After Jalen admitted that she slipped up and gave the number to Alyssa, I warned Destiny you'd probably track her down again." Val pointed at the burner phone on the table. "She was pissed at me, obviously. She's left this behind and hasn't contacted any of us since, and I've no idea where she's gone. She doesn't trust any of us, not anymore. Good work, Buzz. Are you happy now?"

30

That evening, back at home with Alyssa and their children, Eric decided he was going to get drunk. He had a bottle of unopened bourbon in their liquor cabinet, a gift from friends for his fortieth birthday. After slicing off the foil seal, he twisted off the cap and gave himself a long pour in a short tumbler. He carried the glass into his darkened office and eased onto the chair.

He had screwed up everything, and he didn't know how to fix it.

Earlier, Deacon had tried to assure him that setbacks like this were normal, that sometimes family members conspired against others for their own reasons and made it more difficult to track down the missing. But he also reminded Eric, sternly, that Destiny was an adult. She was under no obligation to talk to Eric or anyone else. He suggested that Eric step back for a couple of days and consider whether he wanted to pursue this case any further.

He appreciated Deacon's advice, but what bugged him were the clues he had discovered in Grisby. Clive and Maurice Turner and Lorenzo Cannon. Something was in the works there and it involved Destiny, and he wasn't sure his daughter realized what was going on.

But instinct warned that she was in danger.

The lights in the office brightened. Eric swiveled around to find Alyssa standing in the doorway, a manilla folder in her hands.

"Drinking alone in the dark?" she asked.

"Hard liquor doesn't agree with me." He took a sip of the bourbon, grimaced, set the glass on the edge of the desk. "But I want to black out for another two weeks and maybe when I wake up, all of this will be over."

Alyssa came into the room. An overstuffed leather love seat stood in the corner by the window. She sat on it, the folder lying across her lap.

"Yesterday, I met your ex-girlfriend from college," she said. "Rachel Watts."

"Why is everyone hiding information from me?" Eric lifted the glass to his lips, and this time, when he took another sip, it felt good going down. "Am I a total asshole or something?"

"Come sit, please." Alyssa patted the cushion next to her.

Eric dragged himself to his feet and sat next to her. She shifted to face him, the folder lying between them. She opened it.

Two photographs lay inside, both snapped during his stay at the hospital twenty-one years ago. Eric remembered the pictures, but he hadn't looked at them in years.

"Where did you get these?" he asked.

"An old box in the basement full of your stuff." She smiled. "I've been busy the past couple of days."

"Snooping around behind my back is more like it. You went to see Rachel, huh? I told you I already talked to her. She's not Destiny's mother."

"Check these out again." Alyssa tapped the photographs. "Tell me about these people."

"Obviously, one of them is Rachel. You said you met her."

"Rachel's a lovely woman, and yes, I agree, she isn't Destiny's biological mother." She tapped a picture. "Who is the other woman? The nurse?"

Eric lifted the photograph and stared at the young woman wearing scrubs, standing next to him with a glum expression. He stroked his chin.

"She wasn't a nurse," he said. "She was some sort of assistant, I think. When I finally woke up, she was bringing me food, drawing blood, that sort of thing."

"But she's in a photograph with you," Alyssa said. "That seems significant."

"There is one thing." He set down the tumbler on a side table. "Probably nothing."

Alyssa waited for him to continue.

"She's in the Cannon family," he said. "You know, there's a million of them down in Grisby, right? Her name is Sonya. She was a year behind me in high school. I guess you could say, she kinda had a crush on me back then."

"Go on." Interest brightened Alyssa's eyes.

"After I was discharged from the hospital, I stayed with my grandma for a bit before I went back to college. Sonya turned into stalker chick, for a little while."

"She was obsessed with you?" Alyssa asked. "What did she do?"

"She showed up at the house a few times. She left me these long love-sick letters. It went on for a few weeks."

"Did you tell her to stop?"

"Honestly, I tried to ignore her. I didn't want to hurt her feelings. She seemed sweet, just a tad bit off. I guess because she was with me in the hospital, taking care of me, she felt attached."

"Then it all stopped? Do you know why?"

"I've no idea, but she didn't come around anymore. It's not like I had an argument with her or reported her to the cops." He shrugged. "She just stopped coming around. She must have realized it was a waste of time."

"Do you have any of the letters she gave you?" Alyssa leaned forward. "I didn't find any downstairs."

"If they're still around, I think they might be in my old bedroom at my grandma's house."

"We need to go to Grisby tomorrow," Alyssa said. "I want to see these letters."

"Right." Eric laughed. "Baby, I promise you: *Sonya Cannon is not Destiny's mother*. I never, ever, touched that girl. She was nice, but she was crazy needy, not my type at all."

"I still want to see those letters," Alyssa said. "Humor me, all right?"

Her hands shaking, Destiny entered the familiar number into the new prepaid cell phone. She was about to send the text message she had vowed never to send again.

But breaking things off permanently with Clive had proven to be far tougher than she had thought. She had become dependent on the man, though she hated to admit it to herself. Talking to him, being with him, was like a drug (she knew; she had seen plenty of folks strung out on drugs), and since cutting off all contact with Clive, cold turkey, she had experienced withdrawal symptoms: almost constant thoughts about him and literally a physical *craving* to be in his presence.

Her father said Clive was too old for her. She had thought the same thing when she first met Clive. She was working at a kiosk selling cell phone cases in Lenox Square Mall. Men of all ages hit on her all the time, and Clive wasn't classically handsome. But he had swagger oozing from his pores, and he made her laugh so hard her stomach hurt. Going out with him felt like the most natural thing in the world. Age ain't nothin' but a number, right?

Now here they were, many chaotic months later. She knew he was bad for her, but she couldn't seem to let him go.

She typed into the phone.

Clive its me Destiny. She pulled in a deep breath. *This is my nu cell #. Long story*

She waited a full, heart-racing minute for his reply.

Hey u I missed u girl

Destiny grinned, felt a wave of warmth flow over her.

Can I call u she typed.

Bad time but we can txt

Her fingers raced: *But we have a lot 2 chat bout so much goin on*

Where r u now he asked.

Around ATL

U need 2 get down here 2 Grisby

Destiny frowned. This DNA stuff had become another, recent point of contention between them. Clive had inserted himself in her family matters in a way that she didn't appreciate or approve of, using *Facebook* to track down people she had yet to meet herself.

She typed: *U still there? U know how I feel bout that*

Can u come 2mrw?

Will think bout it

I miss u girl need 2 c u 2mrw

K lemme think K?

Doin this all 4u u will c

Although Destiny had responded that she would think about it, deep down, she realized she had already made her decision.

32

Eric didn't believe that finding a batch of old letters from a lovesick young woman would lead to anything useful, but he was overdue to visit his grandma's home in Grisby. He hadn't been there in over a month. Since his grandma had moved into the nursing home, he and Val had taken turns dropping by the vacant house, usually every couple of weeks. With Destiny's entrance—and recent exit—from his life, Eric had skipped his turn.

"I still think this is a waste of time," Eric said to Alyssa as he pulled his Yukon into the driveway. "Letters or not, Destiny's probably not in Grisby."

"Sometimes to move forward, you first need to go backward," Alyssa said.

"Did you read that in a fortune cookie?" he asked.

Alyssa gave him a long-suffering look. "Trust the process, babe."

It was Wednesday, around noon, and sunny. Eric noted that the ranch home that he and Val had grown up in with their grandparents looked surprisingly good considering its age. His grandparents had built it over fifty years ago, but their family had managed to keep up the maintenance, recently getting the exterior painted and repairing the roof. A local lawn service crew kept the grass trimmed in spring and summer and blew the leaves in the autumn.

The front door crackled open when Eric unlocked it and pushed. The air inside was cool and smelled clean.

Since his grandma had moved out, little had changed. He and Val kept all the furnishings in place, as if in some naïve hope that Grandma Nellie would return home to reclaim the space.

His childhood bedroom was the last door on the left of the hallway. Alyssa followed him as he pushed open the door.

The room was so simply furnished it might have belonged to a monk in a monastery: a double bed standing along the right wall; a nightstand with a lamp; and an old oak desk with a swivel-base office chair. Eric remembered doing high school homework at that desk and probably sitting in that very chair. Still, whenever he came back there, it felt as if he were visiting a TV sound stage that had been the setting for someone else's life. Everything seemed smaller than he remembered.

"I've never really looked in here until now." Alyssa ran her fingers across the bedspread and settled onto the mattress. She nodded toward the closet behind him. "Do we start looking in there?"

The folding closet doors creaked as Eric pulled them open. He hadn't looked inside this closet in many years and wasn't sure what he would find.

He found only empty hangers. Not a single old shirt, hat, or pair of shoes; and certainly, no shoebox of letters.

"It's empty?" Alyssa stood at his side.

"Grandma must have cleared it out. Or maybe I did, when I moved out. I really don't remember. It's been years."

Alyssa crossed back to the nightstand and pulled open the drawer. It slid open with a screech.

"There's nothing in here but dust." She turned to him, eyebrows arched. "Where else can we look?"

"We could waste all day in here. I think we should talk to my grandma and ask if she remembers anything about these letters you're convinced are so important."

"I hate bothering her with this." Alyssa pressed her index finger to her lips, gave him a hopeful glance. "But do you think we can visit her now?"

"She doesn't exactly have a full social calendar these days."

It was a short drive to the nursing home. As they passed the front desk, Eric hoped that Michelle Cannon, the lead administrator, didn't corner him and pepper him with questions about his grandmother's remains; and he hoped, too, that she wasn't aware of the incident at the cemetery. Although it seemed most of the Cannons lived in the area, he wasn't sure how closely they communicated with one another.

Grandma Nellie was napping when Eric entered the room. The television was playing a rerun of an old soap opera, *One Life to Live*, the remote control resting in his grandmother's frail hand.

"We can come back later," Alyssa whispered to him. "Let her rest."

But Eric gently tapped his grandmother's shoulder. "Grandma, it's Buzz."

Grandma Nellie stirred, her eyes fluttering open. A smile spread across her face.

"Buzz? You . . . you . . . you brought your wife." She lifted her arms and reached toward Alyssa.

Alyssa gave her a hug and kissed her on the cheek. "Hi there, lovely lady. I'm sorry to wake you."

"Is it . . . is it . . . my . . . my birthday?" Grandma Nellie asked.

"Your birthday was last month, Grandma," Eric said.

Grandma Nellie cackled. "I know . . . know . . . know my birthday, Buzz! I was . . . was . . . was playing with y'all. It . . . it . . . it . . . gotta be a special occasion for both of y'all to be here . . . it ain't . . . ain't . . . ain't the weekend . . . yet."

"We'd like to talk about Sonya Cannon." Eric pulled two chairs closer to his grandmother's bed. Alyssa settled onto one of them. Eric took the picture that Alyssa had found of him, Rachel, and Sonya and pressed it into his grandmother's hands.

Grandma Nellie raised the photo to her face, squinting despite the bifocal glasses she wore.

"Remember her, Grandma?" Eric asked. "Remember those letters she wrote to me back when I was recovering from the accident?"

"Those . . . those letters . . . yeah." Grandma Nellie glanced at Eric. "That girl . . .girl was crazy . . . crazy 'bout you. Poor . . . thing."

"Do you know where I can find those letters?" he asked. "I went back to the house and looked in my old room, but everything is gone."

"I . . . I . . . I cleaned . . . cleaned out that room long . . . long time ago . . . Buzz. You . . . you wasn't moving back in since . . . since you got you a wife." Grandma Nellie winked at Alyssa.

"Sounds like the letters are gone, then." Eric looked at Alyssa. "We can close that door."

"What do you remember about Sonya Cannon, Grandma Nellie?" Alyssa asked.

"That . . . that poor girl. You know . . . know . . . she passed years ago."

"She died?" Eric straightened in his chair. Alyssa touched his knee, shock showing on her face, too.

"Uh huh . . ." Grandma Nellie pursed her dry lips, remembering. "Way . . . way back."

"How long ago?" Alyssa asked.

"Oh . . . child . . . I." Grandma Nellie laughed, shook her head. "Can't . . . recall . . ."

"Was I still living with you and Granddad?" Eric asked.

"Naw . . . you had moved out." Grandma Nellie touched her forehead as if that would jiggle free the memories. "You started that . . . that job of yours."

"How did she die?" Alyssa asked. "Do you remember?"

"Oh . . . that child took her own life," Grandma Nellie said slowly. "Them Cannons . . . kept it out . . . out . . . out the paper . . . never had a . . . a service. . . or . . . or . . . obituary, neither. They was shamed . . . uh huh."

Guilt surged up Eric's throat like stomach acid. What if Sonya had committed suicide because he hadn't reciprocated her interest? Was his disinterest the trigger for her to kill herself?

He couldn't bear sitting down any longer. He got up and paced, his gut curdling.

"How did you learn all of this, ma'am?" Alyssa asked. "You said they never had a service or ran an obituary?"

"My . . . my friend . . . Ella Mae." She looked up at Eric. "Buzz . . . you. . . you . . . you remember Ella Mae?"

"Vaguely, I think. She lived around the corner from us, right?"

"Uh huh." Grandma Nellie nodded. "Ella Mae was . . . was . . . was married into the . . . the Cannons. She used to . . . used to . . . used to work at the hospital, too."

"Is Miss Ella Mae still alive?" Alyssa asked.

"Child . . . I . . . I don't know . . . but she was . . . she was . . . younger than me."

"Thank you, Grandma Nellie," Alyssa said, and squeezed her hand. "You've been so helpful."

"Where that . . . that daughter of yours, Buzz?" Grandma Nellie asked. "You . . . you found her yet?"

"We're working on it, Grandma."

Outside the nursing home, Eric and Alyssa settled back into the SUV.

"No letters," Alyssa said. Her eyes gleamed. "But that was extremely useful information."

"Listen, Sonya Cannon isn't Destiny's mother," Eric said flatly. "None of this changes that, Alyssa."

"We need to see this through. Let's go talk to Ella Mae."

"Why? I already told you, Sonya isn't the mother. I'm sorry that she took her own life, but I don't see the point of going on with this investigation of yours."

Alyssa's jaw was rigid. "I can go talk to Ella Mae myself then."

Eric opened his mouth to continue to argue—pointlessly, he knew, because Alyssa was like a force of nature when she wanted to be— when he saw a familiar vehicle turn into the parking lot and slide into a spot near the front of the building.

It was Lorenzo Cannon's Lincoln SUV.

"Hey, that's the guy." Eric pointed. "The Cannon kid who assaulted me at the cemetery."

Lorenzo strode along the walkway to the nursing home's entrance. He wore hospital scrubs, like a member of the staff.

"Jesus, does he work here, too?" Eric felt ill.

"He's a big guy," Alyssa said. "You should have called the police when he attacked you."

"The Cannons have a lot of weight in this town. I don't think it would have helped anything. Remember, they own this nursing home, too."

A shadow passed over Alyssa's face. "What's he doing here, then?"

33

Eric and Alyssa waited in their SUV in the nursing home parking lot. Lorenzo had been inside for about ten minutes. Eric didn't feel comfortable driving off until he saw the Cannon kid leave. Perhaps it was a paranoid thought—it was the middle of the day, Grandma surely was safe—but he literally could not make his hands shift gears until he was sure the threat was gone.

His cell phone rang, the call brightening the dashboard display. It was Deacon.

"I've got a hit on the Navigator's tag," Deacon said.

Eric had sent Deacon a text that included a pic of Lorenzo's license tag. It seemed like it might help in Eric's widening search for clues.

"What did you find?" Eric asked. "Alyssa's here with me, by the way."

"The vehicle is registered to the Cannon Corporation," Deacon said.

"Of course," Alyssa said. "They own the funeral home, nursing home..."

"They also own a body broker business," Deacon said.

Eric looked at Alyssa. She was staring at him, too, a curious expression on her face.

"What's a body broker business?" Eric asked.

"They're also called non-transplant tissue banks," Deacon said. "They sell donated human cadavers for profit. I didn't know anything about it either, Newton, until I got the hit on the plate and did a little digging into the Cannon's empire. These body brokers take the cadavers and sell off pieces to interested parties: universities, medical equipment companies that need them for research."

"Morbid," Alyssa said. "But arguably, necessary for science."

"Almost every time I visit my grandma, one of the Cannons working at the nursing home asks me about what we're going to do with her body when she passes," Eric said. "They're super aggressive about it. Like they can't wait for her to die."

"It's extremely profitable," Deacon said. "It's an unregulated industry. Few people know it exists."

Lorenzo exited the front entrance of the nursing home. He walked with a bounce in his step. Eric didn't like that and wondered what this kid had been doing inside.

"This is all interesting, thanks for digging it up," Eric said. "Any news or ideas about my daughter?"

"Personally, I think she's off the grid now, Newton. We'll keep working but prepare yourself for a long wait."

"How long?" Eric asked, knowing it was a futile question.

"Moderate your expectations," Deacon said. "I'll call you with updates."

Deacon terminated the call. Eric watched Lorenzo climb into the Navigator.

Eric shifted into Drive.

"Where are we going now?" Alyssa asked. "We need to talk to Grandma Nellie's friend, Ella Mae."

"I want to follow this dude," Eric said. "No one's seen Clive since he got in this guy's SUV. He knows something."

"Are you sure that's a good idea? He's already assaulted you once."

"It's probably a terrible idea." Eric edged forward as Lorenzo steered toward the parking lot exit. "Let's get after him."

"I'm not comfortable with this," Alyssa said as Eric followed the Lincoln.

"I'm following from a safe distance." Eric sped up as Lorenzo joined traffic on the adjacent road. "I want to see where he goes."

Alyssa quieted, but Eric noticed that her jaws were clenched, as if they had climbed on a roller coaster together and it was about to spin through a loop-de-loop. His own stomach fluttered with butterflies.

He wasn't sure exactly what he would do if Lorenzo led him somewhere problematic, but he would deal with that when it happened.

As it was mid-day, there was only sparse traffic. It was easy to keep the Navigator in sight. It made a right turn, onto a familiar road.

"He's going back to the funeral home." Eric made the turn as well.

"Then you can stop following him now."

But Eric continued to tail him. Lorenzo drove past the funeral home, but slowed about a half mile ahead. He made a left, entering a heavily wooded area.

On a sparsely traveled road such as that one, Lorenzo would be more likely to realize that he was being followed. Eric needed to keep some distance between them.

Eric made the turn as well, onto Candler Road. Trees and shrubbery lined the winding lane on both sides. He didn't see anything through the densely packed trees. It was like driving through a forest.

"Do you know this area?" Alyssa asked. Her hands were locked together in her lap.

"Never been over here." Eric took a tight curve, slowing as he did so. Ahead, the road branched. He paused at the fork.

On the right, a sign declared: *Dead End.* The left branch twisted into more dense forest.

"Any guesses?" Eric asked, drumming his hands on the wheel. "Right or left?"

"How about backwards? I'm not kidding."

"I need to see this through." He turned right. "Let's see where this road ends."

The lane curved sharply a couple of times and straightened. About a hundred yards ahead, a gate blocked the road, bracketed by stacked stone pillars. The gate stood about six feet high, ornately designed from wrought iron. A large, elegantly carved "C" adorned the middle.

He could see, farther ahead and barely visible through the trees, the outlines of a colossal residence.

"The Cannon estate, huh?" Eric asked. "I didn't realize death paid so well."

The Navigator had pulled over to the shoulder of the road, about fifty feet beyond the gate. The vehicle's brake lights glowed in the gloom cast by the overhanging trees.

"He's got to see us now," Alyssa said. "Let's go back."

Eric shifted into Park and climbed out of the truck.

"Eric!" Alyssa said.

Eric shut the door, blocking out his wife's anguished face. He couldn't understand what had taken over him, but he felt an almost feverish compulsion to push forward, to shut down the lies these people kept firing at him. Maybe Destiny wasn't there with them, but dammit, *something* was going on here, and he could not shake the sense that it meant bad news for his daughter.

He approached the gate, dead leaves crackling under his shoes. A cool breeze whispered around him. Although they were a short distance from the commercial district of the town, the area felt as remote as any place Eric had ever been on Earth.

A call box, coupled with a camera, stood on a stacked stone post next to the gate. Eric glanced from the camera to the idling Navigator.

Lorenzo climbed out of the vehicle. Eric felt his sore stomach muscles clench.

"You again." Lorenzo massaged his fist. "You didn't learn your lesson the last time I slapped you down, old man?"

"Where's Clive?" Eric hooked his thumb behind him. "I'm getting this entire conversation on video, by the way. Dashboard cam, kid. If you so much as breathe hard on me, we're calling the police and charging you with assault."

It was a lie, and if Lorenzo was concerned, it wasn't reflected on his face. He wore a look of gentle amusement as he approached.

"How long have you been following me, old man?" he asked.

"Do you make daily rounds of all the nursing homes and other businesses your family owns? What exactly do *you* do anyway?"

Lorenzo had reached the gate. He grasped the iron bars in his big hands and peered at Eric from between them. His dark eyes simmered like banked coals.

"You need to leave," Lorenzo said. "You're close to trespassing. I won't ask again, dough boy."

Eric heard an engine drawing near, glanced over his shoulder. A silver Ford F-150 veered into view. The truck pulled alongside his Yukon, and the driver's side door opened.

Maurice Turner climbed out. He smoked his usual Black and Mild cigar, smoke swirling around his bald head. His sunglasses glinted in the afternoon sunshine.

"What you doin' here?" Turner asked. "You on our asses like flies on shit, man."

"Welcome to the party," Eric said.

"Mr. Newton here is leaving," Lorenzo said. "Care to do the honors, Cousin?"

Turner advanced on Eric. He had about four inches on Eric, and long arms and big hands that reminded Eric of a prize fighter. But the fumes of smoke and alcohol swirled around him; if Eric tangled with him, Eric might win merely because he was sober, and Turner probably wasn't.

"Get on out of here," Turner said. He made a shooing gesture with his hand holding his cigar. "You ain't got no business 'round here."

"You guys are dirty, and you're hiding something about Clive," Eric said. "If it concerns Clive, it concerns my daughter. I'm going to find out what it is if it's the last thing I do."

"Don't nobody care 'bout your nappy-headed girl, man." Turner grasped Eric's elbow, his fingers like steel pinchers.

Eric snatched his arm away. He tossed a look at Lorenzo.

"This isn't over," Eric said.

Lorenzo mimed cocking a trigger and firing at Eric. Eric got back in his SUV.

"I could strangle you right now." Alyssa glared at him. "What the hell was that all about? Some little boys' pissing contest?"

"Just saying what needed to be said." Eric shifted into Drive. "Come on, let's go talk to Ella Mae."

From what Eric remembered, Ella Mae lived around the corner from his grandparents, so he parked in the driveway of his family's house, intending to walk the short distance to his destination. Alyssa had barely spoken to him since they had left the Cannon estate, her eyes simmering. Now, she got out of the truck and waited on the sidewalk, arms crossed over her chest.

"You're coming with me?" he asked. "I don't know if Ella Mae lives around here anymore. Might be a waste of your time."

"Where is her house?" she asked.

Eric pointed toward the intersection. Alyssa started walking and didn't look back.

He knew she was upset with him over his behavior with the Cannon guys. He couldn't blame her. He *was* acting out of character. Usually he kept his head down, avoided confrontations, took only measured risks . . . but this situation with Destiny had triggered a wild streak in him. He wasn't exactly sure what he might do next, and that was a little scary.

It was also exhilarating, if he were honest with himself.

"Hey, babe." He caught up to Alyssa and reached for her hand. "I'm sorry. I've been acting like an ass."

She allowed him to take her hand, but her lips were molded in a firm line.

"Which house is it?" she asked.

"Right around the corner. The red split level with the white shutters. She lived there before she married into the Cannons, moved back in after they divorced. Must be family property."

Although they were holding hands, he had to move fast to keep pace with her. Reaching the house, they advanced down the narrow walkway to the front door.

A black Buick Regal, circa 1990, was parked in the driveway beneath a sagging carport. Potted plants on the verge of disintegrating lined the windowsill.

"Let me do the talking," Alyssa said. "Please."

"You worried I might punch out whoever opens the door?"

"The thought has crossed my mind."

She knocked on the door; the doorbell was nonfunctional, the plastic casing smashed. After waiting for about a minute brought no response, she knocked again.

"No one's home," she said.

But Eric had noticed a fenced backyard with a rusted gate. He stepped toward it. The gate was unlocked, the hinges creaking when he pulled it open.

"Don't go back there," she said. "It's trespassing, Eric. Have you completely lost all common sense?"

"You don't have to come with me."

He entered the backyard. It was a small area, the lawn choked with fallen leaves and thick grass that reached his knees. A tiny patio—a sad square of faded concrete—lay adjacent to the rear of the house, a table with a missing leg standing on it.

A hammock had been erected between two elm trees growing next to the patio. At first glance, Eric thought it was empty. A closer look revealed a man swaddled like a baby within the folds of cloth.

"Excuse me!" Eric said. "Mister!"

The man didn't stir, and Eric had the alarming idea that the guy was dead, that he had stumbled upon a corpse that had been silently rotting away in a ratty hammock. He edged closer and saw the man wore earbuds, the wires trailing away from his head like electrodes.

Eric moved within the guy's field of vision and waved his hand. "Mister!"

The man's eyes widened. Startled, he tumbled out of the hammock and landed on the grass in a knot of limbs.

"Good Lord," Alyssa muttered.

"Are you okay?" Eric asked.

Grumbling, the man got to his feet. He was shirtless, but wore faded denim overalls. He had a head full of gray hair and a beard so thick and matted it could have served as a bird nest.

Snatching out his earbuds, he scowled at Eric.

"Is it time to go already?" he asked. He had a falsetto voice completely out of sync with his grizzled appearance.

Eric glanced at Alyssa. She gave him a clueless shrug.

"Mister, I'm looking for Ella Mae," Eric said. "She used to live here. I thought she still did. My family lives nearby."

"You mean the old woman that lived here?" He scratched his head. "Man, I think she moved to a home."

"A nursing home?" Alyssa asked.

He squinted. Scratched his beard. He glanced at his phone, and his eyes flashed.

"Damn, I'm late for work again." He gathered up a t-shirt that had fluttered to the grass when he fell out of the hammock.

"Wait a minute, please," Eric said. "We need to talk to Ella Mae. What sort of home is she in?"

"Why should I tell you, man?" the guy asked. "You ain't no cop."

"That means I need to pay you, then." Eric fished his phone out of his back pocket. "What's your Cash App handle?"

"Just gimme some cash, bruh. I don't do them apps. They be tracking that shit."

Eric didn't bother asking to whom he referred when he mentioned "they," he simply dug his wallet out of his pocket and extracted the twenty-dollar bill.

The stranger swiped the money with a grin. "Old girl lives in senior living or something like that? It ain't far from here. Like over behind Hardees or something."

"What's your name?" Alyssa asked. "Are you related to Ella Mae?"

"I ain't telling you nothin', brown sugar." He squinted at Alyssa. "You tryin' to get me in trouble with them?"

Alyssa frowned. Eric put his hand on her arm.

"Let's go, Alyssa. I know the place he's talking about."

Walking away from the house Alyssa said, "What the heck was that all for? That guy seemed paranoid."

"I think he's probably squatting there," Eric said. "Anyway, like I said, I know where this place is located. It's a senior living community. Val and I had looked at it for my grandmother before her stroke."

"How did you think to pay that man a bribe?" Her gaze narrowed.

"It's not my first rodeo, unfortunately."

Soon after Eric started driving, he noticed a silver Ford F-150 behind them. He got a glimpse of the front plate: it was a black background, with the word "Blessed" printed in thick white letters.

He felt his stomach twist in a corkscrew.

"Turner is following us," he said.

36

"Why is he following us?" Alyssa asked. Her eyes wide as dinner platters, she turned in her seat and stared out the rear windshield.

Eric squeezed the steering wheel. He felt adrenaline crackling like electricity through his fingers. He looked at the rearview mirror.

"I think I've kicked the hornet's nest," Eric said. "This is purely for intimidation."

"If they're trying to frighten us, they're guilty of something."

"That's what I've been saying." Eric turned onto a road that was off course from where they needed to go, only to see if Turner would follow.

He did.

"Should we call the police?" Alyssa asked.

"It's not illegal to follow someone."

He took a series of turns, totally random, and Turner didn't miss a beat. In fact, he shortened the distance between their vehicles. He was so close that Eric could see the smoke from Turner's cigar trailing from his open window.

"Go to the local police department." Alyssa knotted her hands in her lap, her knuckles bone-white. "Stop this silly game, please."

"That feels like tapping out."

"I don't care what it *feels* like, Eric. We're playing with fire here."

"Maybe you should have stayed home."

Her eyes flayed him. He wished he had bitten his tongue.

"You're right," he said.

It took only a few minutes to reach the police headquarters in downtown Grisby. Eric swerved into the parking lot.

Turner drove past without slowing.

"Thank goodness," she said.

"With our luck, half the police force is probably related to the Cannons," Eric said. "We shouldn't wait here too long."

"Agreed."

He loitered in the parking lot for about five minutes, long enough to be certain that Turner didn't return. Satisfied, he exited the lot and rejoined the flow of traffic. He didn't see Turner's truck again.

They soon arrived at the senior independent living community, Blooming Gardens. He swung into a parking spot close to the main building. It was a large one-story structure with clapboard siding and black shutters. Neatly trimmed perennials and lush, edged grass bracketed the facility.

"This looks very nice," Alyssa said. "Do the Cannons own it as well?"

"Who knows? I assume you want to do the talking in there? This whole visit is your deal. I'm not even sure what we're trying to find out here."

"We need to learn what happened to Sonya Cannon," Alyssa said.

"She died. Tragic, but it has nothing to do with me or Destiny."

"Follow my lead." Alyssa opened her door.

At the receptionist's desk, Alyssa said they were friends of the family there to visit Ella Mae. Eric was prepared to find out that the woman didn't live there, that perhaps she had died, and he was mildly surprised when the receptionist directed them toward the activity room at the end of a long corridor.

He heard salsa music filtering from the room. He exchanged a curious look with Alyssa.

When he reached the wide doorway, he paused. A multi-ethnic group of about a dozen seniors wearing casual clothes danced around a cleared-out area, while salsa groves pumped from a portable wireless Bose speaker. A younger woman, standing at the edge of the dance floor, exhorted the seniors with praise and gentle suggestions as they spun through the moves.

"These folks make me look as if I have two left feet," Eric said. "Wow."

"Do you recognize Ella Mae?" Alyssa asked.

Eric gestured toward the slender, dark-skinned woman who wore a blue Nike jogging suit and sneakers. She was probably the most fleet-footed dancer in the group, spinning and stepping effortlessly with her partner.

Eric wanted to get this over with and talk to the woman, but Alyssa cautioned them to wait until the class concluded. Eric passed the time by checking his phone for messages from his daughter, about the most pointless activity imaginable. Destiny clearly didn't want to talk to him, and Deacon hadn't sent him any updates.

When the class broke up, Alyssa approached Ella Mae, Eric on her heels. The older lady blotted perspiration from her face with a cotton towel.

"You look amazing out there, ma'am," Alyssa said.

"Thank you, dear." Ella Mae had a ready smile, and a voice clear as a bell. She had to be in her mid-eighties, but Eric though she could easily pass for a woman twenty years younger.

"And I know *you*, young man." Ella Mae smiled at Eric. "You're Nellie's grandson, all grown up now. How's she doing? I heard she had a stroke. I need to get by to visit her."

"She's hanging on," Eric said, which was about as honest an assessment as he could offer. "Listen, can we talk somewhere please, ma'am? Somewhere private?"

"Oh, now y'all got this old lady curious." Ella Mae picked up a bottle of water. "Come on, y'all. Walk me back to my apartment."

37

Walking side by side, Eric, Alyssa, and Ella Mae exited the building and went outdoors into the cool, cloudy afternoon. A grid of paved walkways lined with crepe myrtles connected the one-story buildings that housed the apartments. Three golf carts were parked on a concrete slab next to the main facility.

"I stay way over on the other side." Ella Mae motioned with a long index finger. "I could get someone to drive me over there in one of them little golf carts, but I like getting the exercise, uh huh."

Talking to Ella Mae reminded Eric of chatting with his grandma before the stroke had stolen her easy manner of speaking. The two women shared an energy and a perspective that Eric found familiar and comforting.

"It's nice here," Eric said. "Like a city within a city."

"Living here don't come cheap, sweetheart." Ella Mae cackled. "But I always knew how to squeeze a dollar out of a nickel. Comes in handy when you get up into them golden years."

"What do you think of this photo, ma'am?" Alyssa gave Ella Mae the picture of Eric sitting on the hospital bed flanked by Rachel and Sonya Cannon. "Do you remember the young woman on the left?"

Ella Mae stopped in her tracks. She studied the photo underneath a manicured thumbnail.

"Y'all want to talk to me about the Cannon girl, eh?" Her gaze rotated from Alyssa to Eric, and she chuckled. "You know, I used to be married to her uncle Jack. Big Jack, they called him, hah! That silly old fool couldn't keep the snake in the sack, if you know what I mean." She laughed heartily, her eyes shining. "I laugh 'bout it now but when I found out what he was doing, I swear to God, I chased him outta our house with a twelve-gauge shotgun."

"We heard from Eric's grandmother that Sonya took her own life," Alyssa said.

"Sure did." Shaking her head, Ella Mae clucked her tongue. "I know the girl had problems and all, but still—the family was shocked. Right after she was pregnant, too!"

Eric felt a chill ripple down his spine. "When was she pregnant?"

Ella Mae had started walking again, but her gaze kept returning to the photo that she held in both hands. She pursed her red-painted lips. "Must have been about twenty, twenty-one years ago? Yeah, uh huh. I was still livin' with Jack in our house over on South Creek."

"Are you sure?" Eric asked.

"I'm old but I ain't senile—yet." Ella Mae winked.

"What do you know about the baby she had?" Alyssa asked.

"Now, I never saw that child." Ella Mae put her finger to her lips. "I think the family gave that baby away. Don't know if it was a boy, or a girl. A damned shame, what they did. But her mama, Mary—oh, Lord, that woman's a piece of work!"

"Why do you say that?" Eric asked.

"You don't wanna get on Mary's bad side, let me tell you. That woman carries a grudge forever and she's clever. Too clever for her own good. I never liked her." Ella Mae spat on the ground and made a dismissive motion, as if she were expelling the very idea of people like Mary Cannon.

"What did you know about the father of the child?" Alyssa glanced at Eric as she asked the question. Eric felt his face get hot.

"Nothing!" Ella Mae traced Sonya's face in the photograph, and she looked at Eric. "Oh, did I tell you I worked with her in the hospital back when you had that awful accident? Sonya was sweet on you, honey, I remember that!"

"I sort of remember." Eric blushed.

"Acted like she was your girlfriend and all," Ella Mae said. "Had the nerve to get upset when somebody came to visit you. Like she wanted to have you all to herself, uh uh."

Eric didn't know what to say, but he felt his blush deepen.

"Poor girl couldn't keep that job, though. Do you know what she used to do?" Reaching an intersection, Ella Mae paused, looked both ways, and strode forward. Eric hurried to keep up.

"What would she do?" Alyssa said.

"Young lady was a pervert!" Ella Mae said. "I saw it myself, couple times. First time, when I was working the night shift, I caught her lifting a male patient's bedsheet—I think it was Mr. Lee—and inspectin' his plumbin', if you know what I mean. Caught that girl red-handed, I sure did! She flew outta there when I caught her."

Eric felt ill. "She got fired for that kind of behavior? Looking at patients' private parts?"

"Oh, she did more than look, honey." Ella Mae lowered her voice. "Next time, I saw her sitting on a fella's lap while he was out cold. Had her legs wide open." Ella Mae spread her hands as if mimicking what she had seen. "Can't remember his name, but poor man had a stroke and was on a ventilator, uh huh. I told the supervisor what I saw, sure did. That was the last straw, as they say."

Alyssa gave Eric a pointed look, and Eric turned away to glance at Ella Mae.

"They let her go for that, right?" he asked.

"For that, officially? Nope. But I know that's what it was." Ella Mae tapped her temple. "Girl wasn't right up here, if you know what I mean. With her momma being who she was, mean-ass Mary, I kinda understand why that girl was so screwed up."

They had reached Ella Mae's apartment. She asked if they wanted to come inside and talk further and have a glass of iced tea, but Alyssa declined.

"Thank you for taking the time to talk to us, ma'am," Alyssa said. "We won't take up any more of your time. This has been very helpful."

"Right," Eric said. "Thanks."

"What was this all about, anyway?" Ella Mae paused in her doorway, hands on her narrow hips. "I got to runnin' my mouth so much, I didn't ask what y'all was wanting to know about."

"We think we've identified Sonya Cannon's child," Alyssa said.

38

"That's the craziest thing I've ever heard," Eric said, back in his SUV with Alyssa. He started the engine and laughed, but his laughter felt like a jagged blade in his chest. "That isn't how it happened. It can't be. I was in a coma, Alyssa. Totally unconscious. *It didn't happen.*"

Alyssa folded her hands in her lap and watched him, her eyes placid. He hated when she looked at him like that, as if she could probe deep inside the nooks and crannies of his mind and uncover his innermost fears.

"Don't look at me like that," he said.

"Mentally, you were unresponsive. Meanwhile, your bodily functions continued. Breathing. Digesting. Eliminating. Clearly, other physical functions were available, also. It's basic physiology, Eric."

Eric had to lower the window; the pent-up air inside the vehicle seemed to nauseate him. Still, with cool air filtering inside, he felt as if he were going to vomit.

"It didn't happen," he said. "How could it? I would have had a catheter on, remember?"

"Some kinds of catheters can be temporarily disabled. If she were a nursing assistant paying attention, she likely would have known exactly how to do that. She also would have known how to put it back on afterward, and no one would be the wiser."

Alyssa was making too much sense. A sickening shiver passed through him.

"Technically and legally, it was rape." Alyssa glanced at the photograph in her hands. "This troubled young woman took advantage of an incapacitated man."

Eric tried to imagine it, but he couldn't. His mind simply wouldn't allow him to visualize the violation. Maybe that was a good thing.

Alyssa continued: "Sonya conceived—and then, almost certainly, she gave birth at home. A home birth would have allowed her family to keep the child's identity hidden and avoid completing a birth certificate. It doesn't sound as if the family wanted to arrange a normal, legal adoption. I suspect they anonymously dropped off Destiny at a hospital or orphanage in Atlanta, like a scene out of *Oliver Twist*."

"Jesus," Eric said. "What kind of people do that?"

"I'm sorry." Alyssa touched his arm. Her eyes were kind. "This is difficult information to process."

"I remember one of the things she wrote in a letter." Eric shook his head as the memory rushed back to him. "*'I want to have your baby.'* I thought she meant, you know, get pregnant like people normally do, not this sick shit."

"She wasn't well," Alyssa said. "In my practice I see so much untreated mental illness. It doesn't sound as if her mother was willing to get her the help she needed."

"Her mother's a terror, if all of this is true." Eric wiped the back of his hand across his mouth. He closed his eyes and rested his head against the headrest.

He was so tired. He hadn't enjoyed a restful night of sleep in several days. That night, he doubted he would sleep at all.

He opened his eyes and looked at Alyssa.

"None of this information really changes anything," he said. "We're no closer to finding Destiny."

"We'll find her soon. You can tell her the truth about her birth mother. It's going to change everything, Eric."

"I don't want to tell her this story. I'd rather lie and say that Sonya and I had a one-night stand. The truth would wreck her."

"You're her father. Whatever you decide to share with her will be your call. I won't interfere."

Sighing, Eric placed his hands on the steering wheel.

"I don't think I'm ready to go home yet," he said. "Can you call your mom, get her to watch the kids?"

"It's already in the works. Where do you want to go now?"

"I need to wrap my head around things. I feel as if I'm going to collapse like a wind-up toy that's run out of juice. We can go back to my grandma's house and chill for a while. Maybe I'll call Deacon, too, see if he's got any updates for us."

"Whatever you want to do, babe." She squeezed his hand. "I'll be with you."

39

Destiny knew she shouldn't have traveled to Grisby to meet up with Clive, but lo and behold, here she was.

The list of reasons why she should have avoided him was endless: he was emotionally and sometimes physically abusive; she was mired in a toxic relationship with him, like a woman drowning in quicksand; their relationship was volatile and always would be; there was no real future for them as a couple.

Her father had tried to tell her as much, in his heavy-handed way. In her heart, she knew he was right.

But she wasn't ready to let it go. Love—was it love or only her own dysfunctional longings?—drew her to Clive like a moth to a candle.

She was a big reader, always had been. She was sufficiently informed to recognize that she had serious daddy issues. A craving for a father's love had been a hole in her heart for as long as she could remember. Although she had finally connected with Eric, accepting him, with all his quirks and shortcomings, had been a lot harder than she had imagined. Eric was stubborn as hell. He had plans in mind for her. He cared about her, and the commitment he brought to their burgeoning relationship was almost frightening.

Sadly, it was easier to turn to Clive, an older man, a father in his own right, who didn't expect as much of her.

God, I'm so screwed up, she thought. *Like, a textbook head case.*

Nevertheless, the fact was that she had traveled to Grisby to see Clive. They still hadn't talked on the phone, which was odd. All their communication over the past day had been via text messages.

Clive said he was working on major business and had big news to share with her. He promised she wouldn't regret coming to see him.

That was how Destiny found herself sitting at a table in a Chick-Fil-A that evening, sipping a Coke and keeping an eye on the nearby parking lot. She had paid Uber an exorbitant fee to get there from Atlanta. Whatever Clive had in mind had better be worth it.

Will be there at 7, he had texted. *Don't be late, baby.*

As she waited, glancing out the window every minute or so, she read the hardcover of the Octavia Butler novel that her father had given her. Since she was stuck with a cheap burner phone with limited features, it felt like a good time to read an old-fashioned book.

As she sipped her soda, she felt someone watching her. She looked up and saw a woman a few years older than her walking out of the door with a bag of food, her gaze riveted on Destiny as if she had seen a ghost.

Destiny didn't recognize her. She ignored the woman's attention, and within a few seconds, the woman had exited the restaurant. Probably, she had mistaken Destiny for someone else and realized her mistake.

Destiny checked her phone. The clock struck seven.

All right, Clive, she thought. *Where are you?*

She had butterflies in her stomach as she scanned the parking lot. Less than a minute later, she saw his ride.

Here goes nothing.

She gathered her things and hurried outdoors.

40

On the way back to the family home, Eric grabbed take-out from Pop's BBQ. He was in the mood for serious, artery-jamming comfort food.

At the kitchen table, they unloaded the containers: a rack of ribs, rib tips, collard greens, baked beans, French fries, several slices of white sandwich bread. He'd also picked up a six-pack of Budweiser from a gas station.

"You know I never eat like this." Alyssa settled down at the table with a plate in front of her. Eric noted she had selected small portions of each item. "I need to keep my blood pressure down."

"Live a little." He sat across from her, opened the Styrofoam cup of Smokey's special recipe barbecue sauce, and poured it over the rib tips spread across his plate. "For once, I'm not going to worry about my diet."

"I suppose that's why you're drinking non-light beer, too."

"Damned straight." He popped the tab on the beer can, took a long sip, and burped. As he speared a rib tip with his fork and took a bite, a memory struck him like a horsewhip. "Do you know the last time I sat at this table eating food from Smokey's spot?"

"When?" She wiped her fingers on a napkin.

"The day after my granddad's funeral. Someone had brought rib tips to the repast at the church, and a family friend packed leftovers and sent us home with them. I ate them for dinner the next night."

"Food can trigger memories. It's a lot like music, in that way."

"I wrecked my granddad's truck that same night, later on." He chewed, swallowed, washed down the food with another slug of beer. "I never told you what bothered me most about his funeral, outside of the fact that we had a funeral for him in the first place. Did I?"

Alyssa shook her head, her gaze never leaving his face.

He wiped his lips with a napkin.

"I don't think I've ever shared this with anyone," he said. "But it was my granddad's hands that bothered me."

"His hands? What about his hands?"

"He's lying there in his satin-lined coffin, okay? Wearing his best suit, his favorite navy-blue three piece that he liked to wear to church, weddings, whatever. His face looked kind of waxy, but it was still recognizably him." Eric paused. "But his hands . . . baby, I'm not lying, his hands were *too small.*"

Alyssa listened, took a sip of ice water.

"My granddad always had huge hands," Eric said. "He came from a family of sharecroppers, used to work long days in the fields when he was only a kid. After that, he worked tough, blue-collar gigs at factories, warehouses, and so on. Man, my granddad could palm a basketball in one hand as easily as I can palm a grapefruit." Eric stared at his own soft, modest-sized hands. "But those hands Granddad had in the coffin . . . I never forget staring at them and thinking those weren't his hands, they were too small . . . and now we've learned more about this body broker stuff that the Cannons are doing . . ."

"Oh, God." Alyssa touched her chest.

He pressed on: "What if these people chopped off his real hands and sold them, and then sewed on someone else's hands for the viewing? Could they have done that? I don't want to believe it. But it's stuck with me. That's part of what sent me out driving that night I had the wreck. I couldn't get the thought out of my head."

He lowered his head, stared at the food heaped on his plate. But all he could see was his grandfather lying in that casket and those oddly sized hands poking from the cuffs of his suit.

"We can't change the past, babe," Alyssa said.

He felt her fingers on his shoulders, gently massaging. He hadn't noticed her getting out of her chair to stand behind him.

"The Cannon family—they're Destiny's family, I guess," he said in a ragged voice. He sucked in a tight breath. "I don't want her anywhere near them."

Alyssa wrapped her arms around his chest, hugged him tight. He leaned back into her.

"I haven't said it," he said, "but I couldn't do any of this without you. Thank you for being here."

Alyssa slipped her hand underneath his chin and tilted his head upward. She kissed him softly.

"There's nowhere else I'd rather be," she said.

Eric shifted in the chair to face her. She eased onto his lap.

The feel of her body against his, the warmth of her, was far better than any comfort food imaginable. He traced his fingers along her back. He leaned in to kiss her again.

A revving engine, loud as thunder, shattered the moment.

"Who the heck is that?" Alyssa rose.

Eric looked toward the front window and saw a pair of glowing headlights. Someone had parked in the driveway behind his truck.

He nearly knocked over the chair in his haste to get outdoors. Despite the darkening evening, as Eric opened the front door, he could clearly see the visitor was driving a silver Ford F-150.

Maurice Turner.

He thought he could see the glow of Turner's cigar, the metallic glint of a whiskey flask as Turner took a swig.

"Get the hell out of here!" Eric shouted. He waved his arms wildly.

Turner revved the engine again. It sounded as if the vehicle were growling at him.

Eric didn't hesitate, didn't pause to consider the consequences of his actions. He grabbed one of the pavers that lined the flower bed at the front of the house, a hefty stone about the size of a brick, and heaved it toward the pickup truck.

"Eric, no!" Alyssa said.

The paver smashed against the truck's windshield. Eric balled his hands into fists and charged toward the truck. Turner lowered the window. He flung something at Eric that smacked Eric in the face like a flutter of bat wings. Eric reeled backward, startled.

Turner reversed out of the driveway, engine roaring, tires screeching. He bolted like a cannonball down the road.

Eric was so drunk on adrenaline that he nearly chased after the truck on foot. But Alyssa's touch on his shoulder tethered him in place.

He blinked. His heart raced so fast that he felt lightheaded.

"What's this?" She picked up the object that Turner had thrown at him.

He took it from her and brought it closer to the lights that glowed at the front of the house.

"It's a catalog of Cannon funeral home crap." He flipped through the pages and flung it to the ground.

"No," Alyssa said. "It's a warning."

41

Deacon called Eric around nine o'clock that evening with news that Eric immediately interpreted as dire.

We posted a camera outside the house in Duluth where she slipped the net. She came back, Newton, for only a short time, and then she left again earlier today. Haven't seen her since. I think she took an Uber somewhere.

"She's come to Grisby," Eric said to Alyssa when he got the message. "Don't ask me how I know. I can feel it."

He decided to take a drive around town, ostensibly to search for his daughter. Alyssa remained behind at his grandparents' home. She warned him to be careful and to keep his cool.

Keep his cool, right. He had thrown a brick at a guy's pickup truck and smashed the window. He was well past keeping his cool.

Eric went downtown. On a Wednesday night, the streets were so empty that it might have been a ghost town that hadn't welcomed visitors in a decade. If Destiny had ventured out in public there, he would have spotted her from a block away.

Where are you, kid? Eric thought as he cruised the streets. *Who are you looking for here?*

He wondered if she had sought out the Cannon family. It wasn't as though the connection was unknown to her. If Clive had known about Maurice Turner, Destiny would have known, too.

And where was Clive, anyway? What had happened to that loser? None of the Cannons admitted to seeing him, but they were clearly lying. Why?

Before Destiny talked to any of the Cannons, he needed to talk to her first. She needed to learn the truth of how she had been conceived. Eric dreaded that conversation with her, but it was necessary. He owed it to her.

As he neared a QuikTrip gas station, he saw a young woman entering the building. His heart lurched.

Could it be?

He veered into the parking lot, finding a slot in front of the gas station doors. He peered through the windshield, trying to see inside the store.

He couldn't see her from where he was sitting. He went inside. He searched the aisles.

A slender young woman stood at the refrigerator case at the back of the store. She had ebony braids flowing to her shoulders.

"Destiny?" he asked, the name coming out his dry mouth like a frog's croak.

The woman turned to him as she was about to open one of the glass doors. She wasn't his daughter. Not even close.

"Huh?" the woman asked. "You say something?"

"Sorry," he said.

Back in his truck, he clenched the steering wheel, his palms clammy. He needed to decompress. He couldn't go on like this, seeing his daughter in other people, following strangers into stores and making a fool of himself.

He needed to go back home. He had two other children that he had been completely ignoring. Destiny was an adult, and if she wanted to come to Grisby that was her choice. Regardless, it was obvious that she didn't want to talk to him. She would come around, in time perhaps, and maybe they could put this nasty episode behind them.

Come on, you don't believe that, man. You know your kid is in trouble and this town is the last place she needs to be.

"But what can I do about it?" he said, out loud. And realized that now that he was talking to himself, it was further proof of how he was skating too close to the cliff.

His phone rang. He hoped like mad that it was more news from Deacon about his daughter, but when he looked at the display, he found the phone number was assigned to the one contact in his list that he didn't ever want to see late at night: his grandmother's nursing home.

42

According to the nursing home supervisor who called Eric, Grandma Nellie had gone into cardiac arrest late that evening. An ambulance had rushed her to Spalding County West Regional Hospital.

He had seen her earlier that afternoon, and she had been fine as could be expected, talking, laughing, her memory sharp as she recalled events from decades ago. Now, she was on the brink of death.

He couldn't believe it. He picked up Alyssa and they hurried to the hospital. Alyssa called Val, but Val said the nursing home staff already had notified her. She was on her way.

At the hospital, Eric wandered aimlessly in the waiting room. At that late hour, he and Alyssa were the only ones in there. The medical staff was working to stabilize his grandmother, and they wouldn't let him see her until she clawed back from the edge of the precipice.

"It's my fault," he blurted to Alyssa.

Sitting on a hard plastic chair, Alyssa looked up at him with tear-reddened eyes. "What?"

"I pushed them too hard. The Cannons. I was reckless. This is how they take revenge."

"Baby." She shook her head. "Please, no. That's not it."

"What was that psycho kid doing at my grandma's nursing home earlier, huh? They know who I am, and they know who she is. She was a sitting duck in there, they're punishing me—"

"No." Alyssa erupted from her chair and got in his face. Her eyes flashed like steel. "No. This. Is. Not. Your. Fault."

Eric felt hot tears burning trails down his cheeks. He wasn't someone who cried often, and the sensation of the wetness trickling down his face, of the sob bubbling in his throat, felt surreal, as if he were in someone else's body, experiencing someone else's pain. This could not be happening to them, to him, to his grandma. It wasn't her time.

"She's going to pull through." Alyssa pulled him into an almost suffocating embrace. "We need to believe that. We need to pray. She's a strong woman. She's going to make it."

He held onto her, swaying on his feet like a thin tree in a hurricane. After a beat, he slipped out of her arms.

"Where are you going?" she asked.

"I've gotta get some air. Text me, call me if there's a change, whatever."

"I'll be right here. I love you."

He stumbled outside the hospital on weak legs. A cold drizzle fell. He wasn't wearing a jacket and didn't have an umbrella. He couldn't remember where he had parked.

Like a sleepwalker in a fever dream, he shuffled across the parking lot, rain dampening his clothes, soaking him to the marrow. Somehow, he located his truck.

He got inside and started driving.

The hospital was located in a rural area on the outskirts of town. He knew these country roads as well as he knew the lines on his own face. He pressed the gas, cleaving through the rainy night.

He didn't know where he was going. He had no destination in mind. Perhaps if he just drove, fast, when the storm broke, he would wind up in a different time and place, in a better world where grandmothers weren't taken away from their families in the blink of an eye.

He clutched the steering wheel. His hands were damp with rain, with sweat, and with tears from him continually wiping his face.

The road curved precipitously. He swung through the turns at a high rate of speed, the tires grabbing the slick pavement. It was dark out here, with few streetlights illuminating the way. If you were driving as fast as he were, you'd better know the route.

The SUV fishtailed as he navigated a wicked turn. It was heavy as a tank but couldn't escape the laws of physics.

Be careful, a wise voice counseled.

But he ignored that voice and pressed the gas pedal to the floor. A sign warned of another turn coming. He didn't slow.

The SUV whipped through the curve and spun, hydroplaning like a toy car in the middle of the road.

Eric shouted, the wheel spinning so fast it scorched his fingertips. The world twisted crazily, and he had the dizzying sensation of being on a merry-go-round, a carousel in hell.

Around and around and around we go, and where we stop, nobody knows!

The truck rocked to a halt on the shoulder of the road. The headlights shone in the startled face of an immense deer, a buck wearing a mighty crown of antlers.

He had been a heartbeat away from hitting the animal.

A shudder rattled through him. His stomach buckled and twisted, and he vomited on his lap.

"Sweet Jesus," he breathed.

The deer snapped out of its shock and loped away, vanished into the darkened woods like a figment of his imagination.

He had the insane thought that it was the same animal he had narrowly avoided twenty-one years ago, but that was impossible, wasn't it?

He looked at where he had wound up. He recognized the area. His original accident had occurred nearby.

Maybe he had been wanting to come here all along to end his own life, to snuff out his light for good this time.

He lowered the window a few inches and let cool air pour inside. It crystallized the sweat dripping down his forehead.

He rested his head against the steering wheel, shut his eyes. But images strobed through his thoughts: Alyssa's loving face, the beaming faces of his children, Elijah, and Brooklyn. Grandma Nellie's beloved smile.

He saw Destiny's smile, too. A knife twisted through his heart.

I can't breathe around him.

They had gotten off to a rocky start. But he still had a chance with her. He could make up for his missteps. Maybe he'd never be the perfect father, live up to some probably impossible standard he'd created for himself. But he was going to be *there,* dammit.

He had too much to live for to throw it all away.

He lifted his head off the steering wheel, dragged his hand down his damp face.

He went back to the hospital to be with his family.

43

Nellie Newton died the next morning at twenty minutes past six o'clock. Several members of her family were bedside in her hospital room as she peacefully departed this world. Eric was holding her left hand when her spirit eased out of her, and while his grandma had never regained consciousness once the cardiac arrest took her down, he could feel her presence there, with them—and he sensed when she was gone, too.

He kissed his grandmother's forehead. He hugged Alyssa, Val, and his niece, who had come there with Val last night. They had spent hours praying for a breakthrough, but there would be no miracles that day.

As medical staff flooded the room, he shuffled into the corridor on legs that felt as if they were attached to stilts. His eyes were swollen, his tear ducts barren.

He wandered into the waiting room designated for ICU visitors. At that early morning hour, a middle-aged woman was sprawled in a chair. Dark circles ringed her eyes, giving her a racoon-like appearance. She stared at the ceiling as if it contained prophecies of the future.

Eric dropped into a chair on the opposite end of the room. He sat there, staring at the tile floor.

After his grandma's stroke, he thought he had emotionally prepared himself for the inevitability of her death. But he felt flattened with shock, unable to believe it had actually happened.

Grandma's gone...

She had never gotten an opportunity to meet Destiny. He shouldered the blame for that, though he wasn't sure how it was his fault. He felt as if he could have done something to produce a different outcome.

"Who're you here for, sugar?" a woman's voice asked.

Eric looked up. He realized his roommate had directed her question to him, her dark-ringed eyes curious but compassionate.

"I'm here for my grandma," he said.

Rising to her feet, the woman nodded. She clasped her hands in a prayerful gesture.

"I'll pray for your family," she said.

He didn't have the heart to share that his grandma was gone.

"Thank you," he said.

"It's going to be okay. Never give up faith."

She walked past him, but as she did, she stopped and gave his shoulder a gentle squeeze.

Tears dampened Eric's eyes again; he'd thought he didn't have any left to shed. He wiped his eyes, pulled in a breath. He dug his phone out of his pocket. When Val had arrived last night, he had turned it off; it was a distraction from what was going on there at the hospital.

He had multiple voice mails and text messages, presumably from family members and friends who had heard the news about Grandma Nellie. He skimmed the messages and paused on a voice mail that had come in at one o'clock in the morning from a Grisby area code.

The message was garbled, as if the caller had reached him from a sewer, but he deciphered a few words:

"Laronda . . . hotel . . . saw your daughter . . . here in Grisby . . ."

Eric snapped upright in the chair.

Laronda. Yes. He remembered her. She worked at the Days Inn. He had met her at the hotel earlier in the week and she had told him about Clive checking into a room. He had urged her to look out for Destiny, had given her a flyer and his personal cell number, told her to call him and not use the burner phone number printed on the flyer.

Immediately, he tried to call back the phone number from which he had received the voice mail. His call went to an automated message telling him the mailbox was full.

Dammit.

He bounced to his feet and headed toward the door. He almost collided with Alyssa.

"I was coming to check on you," she said. "Where are you going?"

"I need to follow up on a lead." He kissed her quickly. "Be back soon. I love you."

"But the family needs you."

"This is all about family. Someone here in Grisby saw Destiny last night. I promise to tell you more when I get more info."

He was less than a ten-minute drive away from the Days Inn where Laronda worked. He called the hotel from his truck and asked for her. The person who answered said she was on break.

"Is she always on break?" he muttered.

"Excuse me, sir?"

"Never mind."

He pulled into the parking lot and parked next to the Toyota Camry that sat underneath the boughs of a crepe myrtle. Laronda lounged behind the wheel smoking a cigarette and fiddling with her phone.

He rapped on the driver's side window.

She rolled down the glass and squinted at him through a wreath of smoke. "Hey. You got my money?"

"I got your message, part of it got cut off. I tried to call you back."

"I've been workin', honey. You promised money if I gave you information 'bout your girl."

"You mean the reward?"

She rolled her eyes. "Don't act like you don't know what I'm talkin' 'bout." She grabbed a sheet of paper from beside her and waved it at him; he noticed it was the missing person flyer. "How much you gonna give me?"

"Please tell me where you saw my daughter, okay?" He pulled his hand down his grimy face. "I've had a really long night. Please."

Something in his expression must have touched her, because her eyes softened.

"I saw her at the Chik-Fil-A over on Worthington. Looked like she was waitin' in there for somebody, 'cause she kept lookin' outside. I knew it was her, so I watched her for a minute when I went outside. I saw her get in a big truck."

"What did it look like?" His heart thundered.

"One of them Lincoln Navigators, white. I wrote down the license plate for you, too." Her gaze narrowed again. "Now, you gonna give me that money?"

44

Where am I?

That was the first thought that struck Destiny when she opened her eyes. She was lying on something that felt like a mattress. Darkness filled the room, and the only light, a dim, yellowish glow, came from underneath what looked like a closed door, several feet away.

Her mouth was dry as sandpaper, her memory clouded. She had dabbled with enough drugs to recognize that someone had given her something that had scrambled her thoughts.

How did I wind up here?

The last thing she remembered was going to meet Clive in a restaurant parking lot, in Grisby. She'd climbed into the passenger side of the white Lincoln Navigator he had said he would be driving; he'd said via text that the SUV was a loaner, that his Escalade was in the shop.

She had no clear recollection of what happened after she climbed inside, darkness clanging down over her memory like a steel curtain. Only bits and pieces slipped through that barrier: a young man's cruel smile; a woman's whisper—*stay still*—and coldness that rushed like a winter breeze through her blood.

She didn't remember seeing Clive. What had happened to him?

The mattress beneath her felt as if it had been stuffed with rocks. She tried to get up, and a headache corkscrewed through her skull.

She paused, drew shaky breaths. She was still wearing the same clothing: a blouse and jeans. She had her sneakers on, too.

She felt around for her purse, or her phone, and couldn't locate them. It was too dark in the room for her to make out what furniture occupied the space. She could see only dim, bulky shapes.

When the headache abated for a beat, she rose off the bed. She bumped against something heavy and reached out to touch it.

It felt like a cardboard box.

Is this a storage room? Am I in someone's basement?

As if walking across a plank suspended over an alligator pit, she carefully made her way across the room to the door. She found a cold doorknob and twisted it.

It was locked.

"Hello!" she said in the loudest voice she could manage, which was hard because her throat was so dry. She hammered her fist against the door. "Help! Is anyone there?"

She pressed her ear against the wood, listening for a response, for footsteps. But only silence answered her.

She got down on her knees and peered underneath the door. She had only about an inch of visibility. She saw the opposite wall: it was brick. She also saw another door on the other side of the corridor.

"Help!" she shouted, lips at the bottom of the doorway. "Somebody, help me!"

At last, she heard something: footsteps. A shiny pair of black leather oxfords approached and stopped in front of her door.

Destiny got to her feet. She tightened her hands into fists. Whoever opened that door was responsible for keeping her in here like a prisoner. She was going to unleash fury on them as soon as they stepped inside.

"Stand away from the door," a man's baritone voice said.

"Fuck you!" she shouted. "Let me out of here!"

"I've got water for you," her captor said. She heard the soft sloshing of a water bottle. "I know you're thirsty, that's one of the side effects of the sedative. Want the water? It's nice and cold. Step away like a good girl and go sit on the bed."

The mere thought of water made her, inadvertently, lick her chapped lips. Her tongue felt as if it had been cut by a razor.

"Let me outta here!" she screamed.

"Hmm, ok. I'll be back in a few hours, maybe, when you're acting more mature. Water would have been nice, though, wouldn't it?"

She heard his footsteps back away from the door. She surged forward and punched the door.

"Wait!" she cried. "Don't go! I'll go sit down! Please, wait!"

He paused. "Sit."

She obeyed, hating herself, but her body's craving for fluids overrode her stubborn nature.

"I'm on the bed now."

The overhead lights flashed on, searing her vision. She blinked, rubbed her eyes, looked around.

It was a storage room, as she suspected. An empty bucket stood near the bed. What was she supposed to do with that?

She didn't want to think about it.

Stacks of cardboard boxes surrounded her, like pillars. Labels had been scribbled on the sides in black marker: *1990 Funerals . . . 1991 Funerals . . .1992 Funerals . . .*

Funerals? Where the heck am I?

The door opened.

A tall, broad-shouldered young man stood on the threshold. The man with the cruel smile, she remembered him now. Coldness rippled down her spine.

He wore a charcoal suit without a tie. He held a bottle of water in one hand, and a phone in the other. The phone had a distinctive case: an Atlanta Hawks logo taped to the back.

It was Clive's phone.

Oh, God. What had happened to him?

The man smiled at her. "Good girl. Here's your water."

He tossed the bottle toward her, and she caught it. With shaking hands, she unscrewed the cap and drank, savoring the coolness as it splashed down her gullet.

Her captor watched as she drank. He leaned against the doorway, muscular arms crossed over his chest, his dark eyes taking her in but giving away nothing. He radiated a vibe that she recognized: he was one of those guys in the nightclub who would brazenly grab your arm or your ass when you passed, who would ask for your number as if you already belonged to him, who would call you a bitch or toss a drink in your face if you dared to say "no." She had learned to be cautious around such men. Clive, for all his shortcomings, wasn't one of those guys.

She finished the bottle. A belch escaped her.

"Where's Clive?" she asked. "Why do you have his phone?"

A bemused smile flickered across his lips. "Because I'm clever like that. Mama was impressed, too."

Destiny felt as if they were having two entirely separate conversations. Was he listening to her at all?

"Who are you?" she asked.

"I'm Lorenzo Cannon." His eyes narrowed to onyx slits. "Officially, I guess I'm your uncle."

Like a jolt of electricity, the revelation brought her to her feet. "What?"

"But you're nothing to me. You're nothing to Mama. You were a mistake, and the family isn't accepting you now, or ever. If I'd been there when you were born, we would have thrown you in the trash where you belong."

Hot tears blinded her, and she was across the room and in his face without any conscious thought. His insults brought back the worst things she had heard in the many schools she'd attended growing up.

Who are you, girl? You ain't got no real family. Castoff. Mistake. Zero. Nobody.

She tried to hit him, but he grabbed her arms as if she were a child. He shoved her, hard. She staggered backward and dropped to the floor on her tailbone, the impact sending a spike of pain down her spine.

"You and your silly old boyfriend," Lorenzo said. "You thought you would take my inheritance, huh?"

Snarling, he kicked her in the ribs. She yelped, scooted backward away from him.

"I only . . . want to know . . . my family," she gasped. "Don't . . . want . . . your money . . ."

He rushed forward and kicked her again. She tried to turn away, but his shoe connected with her lower back. She shrieked.

Lorenzo grabbed a fistful of her braids in his big hand and hauled her over to the mattress as easily as a man transporting an empty sack. She collapsed on top of it, every breath painful.

"Mama's still thinking about what we're going to do with you." He used a handkerchief to wipe off his hands as if he'd touched something unclean. "You ought to know, she always listens to my counsel. I'm going to be running this family one day soon. I don't need old trash like you spoiling the family name."

He turned on his heel and strode to the door.

"Who . . . who . . . is my mother?" Destiny was in so much pain she barely managed to get the words out.

Lorenzo glanced over his shoulder and gave her that cruel smile of his.

"Her name was Sonya. She's dead."

He slammed the door and turned off the lights.

45

"I got here as fast as I could," Deacon said when Eric opened the front door. "Are you certain this is a good time, Newton? My presence here at your grandmother's house feels inappropriate."

Ten hours ago—it felt like ten *years* ago—Eric had been at Grandma Nellie's side in the hospital when she passed. A dizzying series of events had followed: getting Laronda's message and learning of Destiny's presence in Grisby; fielding phone calls from friends and family who had learned of Grandma Nellie's passing; making new arrangements for the funeral—he and Val had originally planned on allowing the Cannons to handle the arrangements, but there was no way in hell, not anymore, that Eric would let the Cannon family within a hundred feet of his grandmother's body.

With everything that was going on, he hadn't slept since yesterday. He was getting by on too many cups of coffee and nervous energy. Whenever he crashed, he was going to crash spectacularly.

"Thanks for coming." Eric ushered him inside. "Listen, I'm going to get my daughter back."

"You said that on the phone, but with all due respect, Newton, your grandmother passed this morning."

"Do you think I don't know that?"

"Whoa." Deacon gave him a slow-down gesture.

"Sorry." Eric exhaled. "I'll grieve Grandma Nellie when I have my daughter safe with us." He felt a tightening in his chest, as if iron coils were squeezing his lungs, and he had to draw another deep breath before he could continue. "It's what my grandma would have wanted."

Alyssa approached them. Her eyes were bloodshot, and Eric knew she also hadn't gotten any sleep in the past twenty-four hours, but she summoned a smile for Deacon.

"Can I get you anything, Mr. Deacon?" she asked.

"I'm absolutely fine," Deacon said, "and far more concerned about you all. I'm so sorry for your loss."

"Thank you, we're managing." She put her hand on Eric's arm. "He's right, by the way. It's what Grandma Nellie would have wanted. Please help us, however you're able."

"I'm at your service," Deacon said.

Eric led Deacon outside onto the rear patio. A wooden bench table set stood in the shade of a large umbrella. They took seats across from each other.

"All right." Deacon set his briefcase on the table and removed his iPad. "Let's review what we've learned so far and determine our next steps."

"I'm going to the Cannon's estate," Eric said. "I've already decided."

"That's private property." Deacon stared at him, stylus poised over the tablet. "You're not a cop, and neither am I, currently. A police officer would require a warrant."

"Destiny's in trouble. You know that. I don't know why she got in Lorenzo Cannon's SUV. Probably, they tricked her somehow. But that young man is a psychopath. He killed my . . . my . . ." He couldn't go on. He felt a sob bubbling in his throat that threatened to asphyxiate him.

"We can't storm the gates of a private residence," Deacon said. "That's not how I operate."

"I don't care."

Deacon continued as if Eric hadn't spoken: "Now, we can effectively conduct surveillance from outside the property lines. I've the proper equipment for such a task. What we do is this: we gather evidence, we present it to local law enforcement, they get a search warrant. If Destiny's there, held against her will, the proper authorities are responsible for retrieving her. That's how I operate, Newton. I'm a licensed private investigator, not a mercenary."

"Then I wasted my time asking you to come here," Eric said.

"What's *your* master plan, Newton?" Deacon folded his arms across his chest. "Go knock on the front door and demand they let you inside to see if they're holding your kid?"

"I know they're holding her. I'll do whatever it takes to get in there and find her. I'll do it alone if necessary."

"You're a real estate agent, brother. Do you have some search and rescue training I'm unaware of?"

"I'm a father who's determined to find his daughter." Eric stood. "Unless you plan to help me, we've nothing left to talk about."

"Newton, you've got to be the most stubborn sonofabitch I've ever seen." Deacon scowled. Then, he started laughing, a hearty, belly-shaking laugh that drew a frown from Eric.

"What's so funny?" Eric asked. "Do you think I'm kidding? I'm not."

"You remind me of someone I used to know. An old friend. Hated to follow SOP. Believed in following his gut. It got him in his fair share of trouble on the job, but his success rate was off the charts."

"Sounds like you're going to help me, then?" Eric asked.

"I've no choice. I can't have you going up there all half-cocked, can I?"

46

Mary Cannon was exactly where she wanted to be: in control.

She lounged on the leather settee in the grand salon of her chateau. Her butler, Ramon, had poured her a glass of Bordeaux before she dismissed him for the day. She sipped wine and smoked her Parliament cigarette (one a day, no more), the cigarette seated in her vintage silver holder. Although home for the remainder of the evening, she wore a Michael Kors dress, her pearl necklace, and her thousand-dollar Jimmy Choo pumps.

She didn't flaunt her wealth to impress others, although demonstrating your power certainly had its benefits. She enjoyed items of great value—fine wines, designer clothing, expensive jewelry, tony homes, rare delicacies, luxury vehicles—because beautiful things and highly valued possessions brought her immense pleasure by their very existence.

As a woman who had made her fortune in the death industry, she knew better than anyone the transitory nature of the material world. You truly couldn't take it with you. Enjoy it today. Tomorrow is not promised to you.

Her penchant for seizing the day had blessed her immeasurably, personally, and professionally. She had married five times. Mostly, men of considerable means. She had divorced them all and was richer and wiser for the experiences.

Professionally, she was an innovator. She knew this to be true about herself, though she kept many of her innovations confidential. But her bank account testified to her talents.

As she floated on a cloud of self-satisfaction, her baby boy entered the great room. Her heart swelled, as always, when she laid her gaze on him. Such a fine specimen of a young man and so fit to one day assume the reins of her empire.

Mind you, she wasn't planning on dying anytime soon. Her baby was going to have a *long* wait.

It was only fair. It had taken her decades to wrest control of the business away from her father, Big Daddy Cannon, and to stamp out the threats from her conniving siblings. When you were one of seventeen children (twelve boys, five girls) and a thriving family enterprise hung in the balance . . . let's say it gave new context to the phrase, "sibling rivalry."

Twenty-five years ago, Mary had vanquished them all. At seventy-six, she was still the undisputed leader of the family business, the queen bee, the matriarch. Her baby boy would assume control only after her spirit passed through the heavenly golden gates, and not one minute sooner.

"I checked in on the orphan, Mama," he said. "She's got a mouth on her, but I handled it."

"Thank you, baby boy. I appreciate you."

He leaned against the mantel of the marble fireplace. "What do you want to do with her?"

"I'm still contemplating." Mary tapped ashes into a golden ashtray.

"We can't let her stay here."

"Baby boy." Mary gave him a pointed look. "Do you honestly think I would have her live here in Chateau Cannon as a fully-fledged member of the family?"

"Of course not, Mama." He lowered his head, chastened.

"With that said, she's come all this way. Perhaps she deserves some answers."

Her baby boy swallowed. "I disclosed that her mother is dead."

"Then that horse is out of the barn." Mary sipped her wine. "How did she take the news?"

"I didn't wait around to see."

Mary could only smile at him. He had certainly acquired her ways. To deliver a crippling emotional blow and then casually walk away without assessing the damage . . . she had taught him well.

It brought to mind the day she had dealt the finishing blow to Big Daddy Cannon. At the time he was eighty-three, ornery and ailing and worst of all, more misogynistic than ever; he had it set in his mind that her eldest brother would take charge of the family business. Her eldest brother was worthless, but he was a man and the oldest and that was all her daddy cared about—it was what he called the "proper chain of succession." Mary had schemed with their family's lawyer and physician to have Big Daddy declared mentally unfit. She dropped that bomb on him while he lay in his bed, and then she turned on her heel and sashayed out of the bedroom as he hurled curses at her back.

What a fine day that had been.

"Did I speak out of turn?" her boy asked.

"She deserved to know," Mary said. "All that matters is the truth, no matter who speaks it."

"You're so wise, Mama."

She offered her hand. Her baby boy came to her, held her fingers in a gesture of pure love, admiration. She kissed his forehead.

"What if Eric Newton shows up again?" he asked. "He might realize the orphan is here. He's like a bug that won't go away."

She smiled.

"How have we always dealt with bugs, my dearest?"

47

Before he left the house, Eric pulled Alyssa into a tight embrace.

"I'll hold it down here," Alyssa whispered in his ear. "You come back to me, love, understand?"

"I'll come back with my daughter." He kissed her cheek, gazed deep into her eyes. "That's a promise."

"I know you'll keep it." She traced her finger along his jawline, turned to Deacon. "Sir, can you please try to keep my husband out of too much trouble?"

"Copy that, ma'am." Deacon gave her a thumbs-up sign.

Deacon had suggested that he and Eric drive their own vehicles to the Cannon property. Eric suspected that Deacon wanted to save his own neck in case things went south. He couldn't say that he blamed him. This was only a job for Deacon, and he had to live to fight another day. But this was Eric's family hanging in the balance.

After a non-eventful drive, they arrived in the densely wooded area that surrounded the Cannon estate. Eric parked on the shoulder of the road, about a hundred yards away from the front gates. Deacon pulled in behind him.

Eric sat in his truck, his hands clenched in his lap. His pulse raced so fast he felt slightly light-headed. He took a gulp of lukewarm water from the bottle resting in the cupholder. It did nothing to slow his galloping heartbeat.

He recognized with total clarity that this was the point of no return. The last time he had been this nervous he was standing in front of a pastor at a church, about to utter his marital vows. He'd been absolutely convinced that marrying Alyssa would be one of the best decisions of his life, and still he'd been so anxious his knees had been trembling.

He wasn't as certain about confronting the Cannons on their own turf.

What other choice do you have? You know they've got Destiny. Go get her.

He whispered a prayer, and then he climbed out of the truck and met Deacon on the gravel road. It was around six o'clock in the evening. Twilight was nearing, the air growing colder. A breeze whispered through the trees, sounding like chattering, ghostly voices.

"You look apprehensive, Newton," Deacon said. "Getting cold feet?"

"We're past second guessing whether I'm going to go through with this," Eric said. "Have you changed your mind about going in there with me?"

"Negative." Deacon smiled thinly. "Keep the Taser I gave you out of sight. You don't want to antagonize anyone. Remember what I told you about Castle Doctrine in our lovely state."

In the state of Georgia, "castle doctrine" meant that a homeowner had the right to defend themselves against an intruder without facing a criminal penalty. In theory, Lorenzo or any other member of the Cannon family could see him, warn him off, and if he didn't comply, shoot him without facing liability.

"They're going to let me in willingly," Eric said. "We're going to have a nice, friendly chat."

"Doubtful, but remember, I'm tracking you, and I'm listening. No matter what goes down, I'll know where you are and what's happening."

Deacon had attached a dime-sized GPS tracker to the inner cuff of Eric's jeans and tucked an equally miniscule audio bug inside Eric's shirt collar.

"Let's hope none of that's necessary," Eric said. "But it's a good back-up plan."

"Let's get to it then."

They shook hands. Deacon waited behind while Eric approached the front gate.

Let's do it.

At the call box on the stone post, Eric pressed the "Call" button.

"What do you want, Mr. Newton?" It was a woman's husky voice that he identified as the matriarch herself, Mary Cannon.

"My daughter is here," Eric said. "I've come to bring her home."

"You're not welcome at Chateau Cannon, sir. Kindly leave."

Chateau Cannon? Was this woman serious?

Eric stepped closer and leaned in, his mouth so close to the speaker he could have kissed it.

"I know all about Sonya," he said. "It's time we clear the air."

About a minute passed without a response, Eric's heart pounding so hard that the ground beneath him seemed to shift and throb in sync with his heartbeat.

Then the gate buzzed open.

48

The Cannons easily had the most palatial residence in the entire town. Before coming, Eric had studied an aerial view of the property on *Google Maps* and estimated their spread covered six or seven acres. The actual breadth of the mansion they had constructed on the land was breathtaking when viewed up close: it looked as if they had transported a chateau from the French countryside and dropped it onto a massive plot of cleared out space in the Georgia backwoods. The realtor in Eric was calculating how much this place would bring on the market and wondering if the interior were as impressive as the outside.

A walk of a hundred yards or so took him along the paved lane to the wide staircase that ended at an ornately crafted pair of doors. No one stopped him from approaching, and he didn't see any vehicles. Another blacktopped lane twisted around the side of the mansion, probably to a garage where he found find the Navigator.

His palms were cold, clammy. He climbed the staircase and pressed the doorbell. The series of chimes sounded like a tolling bell in a cathedral.

He glanced over his shoulder. He couldn't see the gates from where he stood. It was as if passing through the entrance had dropped him down a rabbit hole and left him in some unknown place.

Could Deacon still track him? Would he be able to hear him?

It hadn't seemed like a worthwhile topic earlier, but there, standing on the threshold of the lion's den, Eric felt his nerve faltering. He had made it this far on too much caffeine, bravado, and sheer desperation. He wasn't sure he had anything left in the tank.

The door opened. Mary Cannon loomed inside; she looked taller than the last time he had seen her, as if his thoughts of her had increased her size. She beckoned him forward with a bejeweled finger.

"Good afternoon, Mr. Newton." She spoke with the same solemnity that she probably used when addressing those who came to her funeral home looking to purchase services and plan memorials, a melancholy tone that was so dramatic it had to be rehearsed.

"Thanks for letting me in." Eric crossed the threshold. "I don't want to intrude, ma'am, but I need to find my daughter."

Mary wore an expensive-looking crimson dress that flowed all the way to her ankles, a strand of pearls that rested on her broad bosom, and heels that gave her a three-inch height advantage over Eric. He never would have considered her attractive, but she carried herself with the self-assured presence of an actress accustomed to stealing every scene she inhabited.

"Come have a seat." She gestured with a broad sweep of her long arm.

The entry hall was enormous. It had a marble floor and a grand spiral staircase, a huge crystal chandelier that had to be worth a fortune. Massive oil portraits of people who looked like family members decorated the walls, but the biggest portrait in the corridor was a masterfully rendered painting of Mary Cannon herself.

"Impressive residence," he said. "I didn't know the funeral business could be so profitable."

She responded with a haughty toss of her long black hair (surely a wig, he thought), and downturned lips. She strode forward without waiting for him, her dress flowing around her like soft wings. Her walk was so smooth she might have been gliding. He followed.

She led him into an old-fashioned salon. The gigantic room had a cathedral ceiling, heavy draperies hanging on long windows, wallpaper threaded with gold filaments, more marble flooring, and a fireplace vast enough to roast a wild boar.

Lorenzo waited inside, too. He was propped against the fireplace mantel like a silent sentinel, his eyes twin pits of emptiness.

Eric felt his muscles tense. *Here we go.*

"You've already met my baby boy," Mary said.

Baby boy? Right.

"We've crossed paths," Eric said.

"Indeed." Mary settled onto a large settee and beckoned for Eric to sit across from her in an overstuffed chair. A glass coffee table standing between them held a pack of cigarettes, a lighter, a gold ashtray with an extinguished cigarette balanced on the edge, and a goblet of dark red wine that suggested freshly drawn blood.

"Let's get down to business, Mr. Newton." She crossed her long legs. "I'm a busy woman and I don't waste time with pointless formalities."

"Fine. I know all about Sonya." Eric balanced on the rim of the chair as if sitting on a knife edge, angling himself so he could keep a watch on Lorenzo. "She's the mother of my daughter. She took her own life. I was sorry to find out about that."

"My dear daughter had her challenges." Mary spread her hands; she had sparkling bracelets on both wrists, glimmering rings on every finger. "I tried to talk to her, but it was to no avail. Then I learned she was pregnant—by you."

"It wasn't planned." Eric shifted on the chair. "I was in a *coma.* Did she ever tell you that?"

"My daughter told me everything." Mary tilted her head haughtily. "But how did you piece this together?"

"I've got my sources." He cracked his knuckles, a nervous gesture, but he couldn't help it. "You put Destiny up for adoption. Why? You obviously could have taken care of her." He gestured to the trappings of wealth surrounding them.

"I don't owe you an explanation. A simple man like yourself would hardly grasp my motives."

Eric ignored the insult. "Listen, where is she? I know y'all picked her up last night."

Lorenzo stirred, but didn't speak. He seemed deferential in his mother's presence, like a muzzled pit bull.

"That young lady has caused a lot of headaches for me." Mary plucked the pack of cigarettes off the table. She slid one out, fitted it into a vintage holder, lit it, and took a long drag. "I rarely smoke more than one cigarette a day, but this matter deeply troubles me."

Eric waited for her to continue.

"Her boyfriend came here to my town." Mary's lips puckered. "He's some two-bit hustler back in Atlanta. He contacted my nephew and seemed to believe he could run a hustle on me." She laughed, a hollow sound. "Hustle. Me."

Lorenzo snickered. Eric had to ask, though he dreaded the answer to the question.

"Where is Clive now?"

"Gone." Mary exhaled a ring of smoke.

"Gone where?" Eric asked.

"Wherever little men wind up when they encounter a greater foe," Mary said. "Now this young lady has come, too, perhaps hoping to lay her hands on what she believes is her share of the family fortune."

"She wants to know about her mother," Eric said. "She doesn't want money, especially your dirty money."

"Dirty money?" Mary asked.

"You guys are like a funeral mafia. I know about the body broker business or whatever you call it. Every time I went to visit my grandma, one of your family minions was pestering me about donating her remains when she's gone. So you can sell off pieces of her body to the highest bidder."

"That's a legitimate business, Mr. Newton." Mary scrutinized him though a screen of smoke. "We provide only services and products that our business partners desire."

"You won't be selling off anything from my grandma. We've moved her funeral away from your family to a competitor, Bradshaw and Taylor."

"I'm sorry to hear about Nellie's passing," Mary said. She managed to sound regretful, if only for a moment. "She was a dear woman. A valued customer." Mary threw a look at her son, Lorenzo. "We took excellent care of Mrs. Nellie Newton, didn't we, child?"

"Only the finest care." Lorenzo smiled his shark's grin.

Eric was suddenly so cold that a winter breeze might have slid into the room and wrapped its icy fingers around him. He erupted to his feet and glared at Lorenzo.

"You killed her, didn't you, you sonofabitch?"

The kid moved cobra quick, so fast that Eric didn't have time to respond, couldn't defend himself. Lorenzo lunged forward and hit Eric in the face with a straight right punch. Eric's head snapped back, and he literally saw stars.

Nobody's ever hit me like that . . .

The next thing he knew, he was lying on the floor. He must have knocked over a vase as he fell, because random jagged shards surrounded his head like a crown.

"Oh, dear," Mary said, but she sounded amused, not the least bit upset. "Look at you boys, breaking things in the house."

Eric's jaw felt as if might have been broken. He tasted blood.

Dizzy, he tried to get up.

He suddenly felt a pair of strong hands on him like hooks, hauling him upright. He smelled cigar smoke and whiskey.

"This cat ain't learned his lesson yet, huh?" Maurice Turner said. "You owe me for cracking my goddamn windshield, sucka."

Eric hadn't realized the man was lurking nearby. Turner wrapped his arm around Eric's neck. Eric tried to break his hold, but Turner's arm was like a steel coil. He dragged Eric to his feet.

"Hold him still, cousin." Lorenzo massaged his knuckles.

"Deacon, help!" Eric shouted, blood spraying from his lips. "They're gonna kill me!"

"So dramatic." Mary took another drag on her cigarette, her eyes glittering like the multiple pieces of jewelry she wore. "Do your thing, boys."

Lorenzo smashed a fist into Eric's stomach. Eric gasped and folded over. Turner jerked his head upright again.

"You gonna take this ass whippin'," Turner said. "Keep ya head up and take it like a man."

Eric tried to throw off his grip, but he was too weak, in too much pain.

Lorenzo juggled his big fists like a boxer. His eyes glinted.

"I did the deed on your granny, by the way," Lorenzo said. "My first time giving the dose. It had to be her." He grinned.

Eric shouted. Lorenzo hit him with a jab to the kidney. Eric choked on a strangled cry. He felt his knees give out, his insides boiling over.

Turner flung him to the cold floor like a discarded sack of second-hand goods. Eric tried to get up. Turner pressed his boot against the back of Eric's head.

"This cat don't wanna quit, does he?" Turner laughed. "Got you some heart, huh?"

Eric groaned, his bloody mouth mashed against the floor.

"Only . . . wanted . . . my . . . daughter . . ." Tears flooded his eyes.

Lorenzo knelt so that Eric could see his face.

"I guess you didn't know that we own Bradshaw and Taylor, too." Lorenzo smirked. "Yup, we got your precious granny right now, old man. We're gonna butcher her like a hog and sell off every itty bitty little piece of her."

Eric screamed. He thrashed. He saw himself throwing off their arms, swinging his fists and knocking them all down like bowling pins and charging through every room until he found his daughter.

But that fantasy died when they rolled him over onto his back and Lorenzo pinned his shoulders to the floor, immobilizing his arms.

"Hold him still, cousin," a feather-light voice said.

A woman's face floated above Eric. His heart clutched. Her resemblance to Sonya was uncanny, and she wore scrubs, too.

He was losing his mind. *It can't be Sonya, she's dead . . .*

"Sonya . . ." he gasped.

She smiled, but the smile didn't reach her eyes. Her large brown eyes were empty as a jack-o-lantern's.

"Sorry, I'm Angel," she said. "Go to sleep now, sweetheart."

A needle punctured his neck.

49

Somewhere on the floor above her, Destiny heard a man screaming.

Eric, she thought. *Oh, God.*

Her father had come there to find her. She knew it as well as she knew the sun was going to set that night. He was as relentless as a force of nature, but she feared that in the Cannon family, he was butting heads against a more formidable force.

Her body ached from the punishment she'd received from Lorenzo. The young man was a psycho, utterly terrifying.

It was equally horrifying to discover that he was a blood relative. Her uncle? Sickening. What were their family reunions like?

And Clive . . . God, she wished Clive had listened to her and stayed out of her business. But her boyfriend couldn't resist a chance to run a hustle on someone, to find some angle to siphon cash out of someone's pocket. He was a con artist to his core, but she feared he wasn't going to be running any more games.

She sat on the mattress hugging herself, her cheeks damp with cold tears. She had been locked in that room, sitting in the dark, for what felt like weeks, but she guessed it was really about a day. They hadn't fed her and hadn't let her out to use the bathroom, either. She'd had to do the deed with the bucket they had given her, which she had left on the other side of the room after she had used it.

She realized the screaming had stopped. She didn't know what that meant, but her gut told her it was bad.

Sometime later—maybe twenty minutes or so, she wasn't sure since she had no way to tell time—she heard footsteps approach the doorway.

She straightened. *I've got to get out of here.*

Had that really been her dad screaming? If so, she needed to get help for him. She needed to get help for both of them. If she could get her hands on a phone, maybe an old school landline, she could call the police.

She pushed onto her feet. Her muscles tensed. Adrenaline had kicked in, blunting the pain from the punishment she had endured earlier.

The lights flickered on.

Destiny edged across the room, her sneakers whispering across the floor.

When the door swung open, she didn't hesitate: she bolted.

Lorenzo's eyes widened and he gave a small "hey" of surprise. She flashed by him like a dark streak and raced into the corridor.

He laughed. "You're not going anywhere."

She didn't remember being brought into this place. The hallway was wide enough to fit a truck. It had recessed lights, brick walls, a dark stone floor. Large oil portraits hung on the walls, spaced at regular intervals.

What was this place? She didn't recognize any of the people in the portraits. They had faces of varying shades of brown. Some kind of museum?

Big metal doors occupied the spaces underneath each piece of artwork. But the doors were too small for anyone to pass through them—unless you crawled inside . . .

Crypts, she thought, and then realized that had to be wrong, because it was just too strange, too bizarre for her to be inside catacombs or somewhere crazy like that.

The hallway was long, like an endless corridor in a bad dream. She saw a staircase at the end, winding upward into the shadows.

Lorenzo's footsteps clapped behind her. He was running, too.

She reached the staircase and took the twisting steps two at a time, her legs catapulting her as if they had springs in them. At the top of the steps, she shouldered open a door.

A petite, brown-skinned woman stood just outside the doorway. She wore hospital scrubs and white shoes. Her silver name tag said: Angel Cannon.

Was she another relative of hers? What was this place? A hospital? Nothing made any sense.

"I need help," Destiny said. "Please, call the police."

"Hmm, another one," the woman said. Her eyes were flat as faded pennies.

"Please," Destiny said.

The woman pointed to Destiny's left. By reflex, Destiny turned to look.

A sharp, tiny object pierced Destiny's neck. It felt like a mosquito bite.

A needle, Destiny thought. Sluggishness came over her, her legs folding. *They got me again . . .*

Angel caught the unconscious young woman before she dropped to the floor.

50

Eric woke with a shudder into darkness, a breath lodged like a glass shard in his throat.

Where the hell am I?

It was so dark he wasn't sure he was actually awake. Was he dead? If he were dead, would his heart be hammering so hard? Would his body be fractured with pain?

Not dead. Not yet.

Wherever he was, he lay flat on his back. He couldn't move his hands. His arms felt as if they were bound against his legs with cords.

No.

He smelled wood and his own sour sweat. The coppery taste of blood lay on his swollen tongue.

He tried to get up. His head banged against something; it felt like a lid. He tried to turn on his side, and his shoulders bumped into an immovable object. He had no range of motion at all.

Comprehension washed over him in a terrifying wave.

The family of morticians had put him in a coffin.

"Help!" he said, and it hurt to speak.

He heard the hum of an engine, felt the coffin vibrating. Someone was transporting him. Who? To where?

He couldn't remember how he had wound up in there. He remembered a woman who looked eerily like Sonya hovering over him —*Sorry, I'm Angel,* she'd said—and then she injected him with something, shuttling him into darkness.

Pain pulsed in a hundred different areas of his body. He felt dried blood crusted like glue around his nostrils and lips.

While he was unconscious, they must have tossed him into this thing. He realized he was breathing too fast, the ragged sound of his breaths like a bellows in the enclosed space. Two years ago, he had injured his shoulder and his physician sent him to get an MRI. Lying in the bore of that noisy machine for twenty minutes was the closest approximation to being trapped in the coffin, and those twenty minutes had felt like an eternity.

Sometimes, you didn't realize you were claustrophobic until you were trapped in a box.

His breaths whistled out of his nose and parched lips. He had to calm down. He had to *think*.

He had to get out.

Destiny needed him. He didn't know if she was still alive, but he wanted to believe she was there at the Cannon estate, subdued against her will. Those psychos would have told him if they had killed her.

Just like they had revealed what they had done to Grandma Nellie.

I did the deed on your granny, by the way. . .

The memory of Lorenzo's cruel, smirking face triggered a fresh rush of fury that boiled like oil in his blood.

He had promised Grandma Nellie he would bring his daughter home. Now, that promise meant everything.

He bent his legs. Moving was difficult because of the bungee cords wrapped around his legs, but he felt his knees brush against the lid. The lid shifted, almost imperceptibly, and he saw a slice of light at the edges of the box.

"Help!" Eric shouted again. This time his voice was louder.

"Hey, settle down back there, man."

It was Turner. His voice was loud, syrupy at the edges.

Turner said, "We got only a short ride to where I'm taking you."

"Help!" Eric shouted again.

Turner switched on some music and cranked it up. The bassline rumbled like an earthquake through the coffin. It was an Isley Brothers song, "Footsteps in the Dark."

Eric's mind raced. If Turner were driving, that meant they were probably in the hearse. A short ride from the Cannon estate meant they were headed to the funeral home.

Why the funeral home? Eric thought about the equipment they housed there and felt a nearly paralyzing bolt of terror nail his heart.

The crematory.

He was willing to bet that Clive had met the same fate. *Gone,* Mary had said with an exhalation of smoke.

He didn't feel his cell phone on his person. They must have taken it. He wouldn't have been able to reach it, anyway.

Was Deacon still tracking him via GPS? Had he listened to what had gone down back at the house? Or had they gotten to him, too?

"Deacon, hey," Eric said, trying to direct his voice into the bug that he hoped was still attached to his shirt collar. The music in the hearse was so loud he worried it would muffle his words. "I'm in a box . . . they're taking me to the funeral home . . . the crematory . . . get help, man!"

He bumped against the lid as the vehicle clanged over a pothole. The impact exposed another small gap between the lid and the base of the coffin.

He raised his legs as if doing a leg lift. What looked like a length of bungee cord held the lid in place. But he couldn't get enough leverage to force it open.

Suddenly, the vehicle's engine cut off, the music dying. Dead silence settled over him.

Eric's pulse quickened. A door opened, slammed shut. He heard shuffling footsteps dragging along the side of the hearse.

Turner was sinking deep into his cups tonight. The man was clearly a functional alcoholic. Functional enough that his family trusted him to transport a living person to the crematory and shove them into the furnace.

Eric heard the rear cargo door of the hearse creak open. Turner hummed to himself, a song that Eric recognized as the last few notes of that classic Isley Brothers jam.

"Hey, I've got money," Eric said. "You let me out, I'll pay you."

Turner chuckled. "Aw, shit. This is family business. You ain't got enough money to pay me off, Negro."

Turner shuffled away. Eric heard what sounded like a garage door opening.

About a minute later, he heard another machine. He had no idea what it was, but it grew louder as Turner brought it closer.

What sounded like metal arms scraped along the bottom of the casket. A forklift?

"Help!" Eric shouted, but knew it was pointless.

The machine extracted the casket from the hearse. Eric lifted his legs to bump the lid, and in that narrow wedge of visibility he saw only the vast night sky and cold, distant stars.

He heard wheels grinding across stone as the forklift transported him. It placed him atop a solid surface. The whirring metal arms retracted.

As the forklift grumbled away, Eric rocked hard to his left. The casket tipped a few inches, but crashed back onto the platform. Eric gathered his strength and rocked to his right. He imagined himself as a log rolling downhill. He roared and strained and rocked side to side.

Do it . . . do it . . . do it . . . now!

"Hey!" Turner shouted.

Eric felt the coffin tip sharply to the left, suspended in air—and then he was in a stomach-flipping free fall. The box fell and crashed against the floor. His head banged against the lid. He saw blackness for a second, fought to keep his hold on consciousness.

"Goddammit!" Turner yelled.

The top had popped off the coffin. Eric gasped, sucked in warm air.

Rolling onto the floor had knocked loose the cords binding his arms, too. The cords flopped around him like dead tentacles. Mashed against the floor, he groaned and raised his body as if doing a push-up.

He crawled out of the coffin.

Turner stumbled toward him. He grasped a whiskey flask in one hand. His eyes were bloodshot, face glistening with sweat.

Large machines sat in the shadows like dozing beasts. The crematory's incinerator hummed, wide maw open, like a shark's mouth waiting to be fed.

As Turner shambled toward him, Eric flicked out his arm—his muscles hurt like hell—and snagged the cuff of Turner's slacks. He jerked.

Turner pinwheeled his arms, lost his balance. His flask tumbled through the air. He staggered and dropped to his knees.

"Dammit!" Turner cursed.

Bungee cords were still wound around Eric's legs. Scrambling like a sand crab across the floor, Eric flung a wild punch at Turner's head. His fist connected with Turner's jaw. Turner's head snapped to the side, and his tongue lolled from his lips.

Eric rolled onto his back and grabbed the cords from around his legs. He unlatched them, tossed them away.

He heard the rumble of an approaching vehicle approaching, saw the glare of headlights. His heart clutched. Was it that damned kid Lorenzo not trusting his drunk cousin to do the job?

A car door opened, and a familiar basso voice spoke.

"Looks like I got here right on time, Newton," Deacon said.

51

Working together, Eric and Deacon strapped a protesting and deeply inebriated Maurice Turner to a chair in the crematorium, using the same set of bungee cords the Cannons had used to restrain Eric in the coffin.

Beyond the building's large garage-style door, the night was empty and tranquil. Eric guessed they were on a piece of funeral home property used only by staff, and at that evening hour, no one was working.

"I wondered when you would show up," Eric said to Deacon. "These guys beat the living shit out of me back there."

"I experienced a temporary crisis of indecision," Deacon said. "I'm operating outside of my professional responsibilities now."

"One dad supporting another, huh?" Eric said.

"You got out of that predicament on your own." Deacon nodded toward the tipped-over coffin lying on the floor. "Nothing can stop a man who refuses to quit. Keep that in mind, Newton."

Meanwhile, Turner spat slurred threats at them.

"I'ma kick y'all asses, man." Turner tugged at the cords. "Soon as I get up outta this chair. Y'all asses is mine." He kicked toward Eric, his black oxford missing Eric's shin by a wide margin. "Next time, I ain't gonna miss, sucka."

Deacon delivered a back-handed slap to the man's face. Turner winced, his bloodshot eyes swimming into focus.

"Where's the young lady?" Deacon asked. "You know the woman I'm taking about, sir."

Eric could see the machinery churning in Turner's whiskey-soaked mind.

"Don't lie to me," Eric said. "I know she's at the Cannon house. Is she held against her will? Where in the house are they keeping her?"

"Hmph." Turner spat a stream of dark blood at Eric's feet. "I ain't no little bitch. Kiss my black ass."

Eric looked at Deacon.

"What're you thinking, Newton?" Deacon flashed a hard grin. "A lightbulb went off in your eyes."

"This dude here was going to cremate me. Like they did to Clive."

"Hey, man," Turner said, "you can't prove none of that shit."

"I know you did it. You were all set to burn me down to a heap of ash, too." Eric pointed at the massive furnace; he brought his finger back to Turner. "Now, when I ask you about my daughter, you tell me to kiss your ass."

"Takes a helluva lot of nerve, doesn't it?" Deacon sighed. "I regret that it's come to this, but I think you know what we need to do."

"Let's do it," Eric said.

They seized the back of the chair in which they had bound Turner. They started to drag it across the floor toward the incinerator's platform.

"Hey!" Turner bucked against the cords. "Hey, man!"

They slid Turner another foot closer. Eric approached the machine and studied the various knobs and buttons.

"This doesn't look that complicated." Eric pressed a button. He heard a tremendous whoosh of flames deep in the depths of the machine and felt a wave of heat.

"Hey, brothers, look!" Turner's head, shiny with fresh sweat, swung from Deacon to Eric. "We ain't gotta do this!"

"Where is my daughter?" Eric said, hand poised over the machine's control panel. "I'm not asking again."

"They got her down in the catacombs!" Turner bobbed his head like a doll. "Way downstairs in the crib, man. I ain't lying!"

"Of course, a family that made its fortune in death would have catacombs in their house." Eric came around the chair and stared at

Turner. "Now, exactly where are these catacombs, and how do I get in there without anyone noticing me?"

52

Deacon kept a first aid kit in his Jeep. He opened it and offered Eric packets of antiseptic wipes and ibuprofen.

"You look like you've been in a mixed martial arts match," Deacon said. "On the losing side."

"I'm not feeling much pain right now." Eric clenched and unclenched his hands. "I'm ready to go wrap this up."

"You're high on adrenaline. When you crash, the pain is going to flatten you. I speak from experience, brother."

Eric cleaned blood from his face with the wipes and dry swallowed a palmful of the tablets.

They were standing next to the hearse. Eric had the key to the vehicle, which he had found by rifling through Turner's pockets. He found that Turner had stashed his cell phone in the glove compartment, clearly planning to destroy it off-site after he had disposed of Eric.

Alyssa had sent him two text messages since he had left her at the house, asking about what was going on. He responded that he was okay, that things were looking up.

She'd be justifiably furious with him if she knew what had really happened and what was to come.

Eric turned to Deacon. "You aren't going back there with me, are you?"

"I've already violated my code of conduct."

"Can you stay here and keep an eye on Turner? Make sure he doesn't slip away and warn them that I'm coming?"

"He's not going anywhere." Deacon indicated the crematorium's open door; Eric could see Turner strapped to the chair, chin slumped against his chest as if he had dozed off. "I'll give you thirty minutes. Then I'll need to take corrective action."

"You mean call the cops?" Eric asked.

Deacon said nothing, his hawk-sharp eyes offering no answers, no promises.

"I get it, it's your job," Eric said. "But like I told you before, this is my life."

"Be careful with that piece you found, Newton."

When searching the glove compartment, Eric had also discovered a .38 revolver. It was fully loaded. He decided to keep it. Back at the estate, they had stripped him of the Taser.

"You mean the gun?" Eric hadn't disclosed his discovery to Deacon. "I know how to use a firearm. Even took lessons."

"If you aim it at anyone," Deacon said, "you'd better be ready to pull the trigger and you'd better have a damned good reason for it."

"Noted. We'll be in touch."

Eric climbed into the hearse. It was perhaps the most surreal conclusion to a day straight out of an epic nightmare. That morning, about fourteen hours ago, he had been holding his grandma's hand when she slipped out of this world. That evening, he sat behind the wheel of a stolen hearse with a foolhardy plan to rescue his daughter.

The steering wheel was wrapped in a faded, leopard-print cover. Something out of Turner's personal collection. Who would have thought to personalize such a hearse?

An air freshener danged from the rearview mirror, but the interior smelled of spilled whiskey, sweat, and cigar smoke.

Deacon waved as Eric drove away. Steering the hearse felt like captaining a boat, and he was careful to watch his speed.

Turner had said that the Cannon estate had an alternate point of entry, accessible via a different road. He approached the property from the rear, bumping along the gravel lane. A modest gate stood ahead, chain link glimmering in the glow of the wrought-iron lamp posted nearby.

He parked, got out. At the gate, he found the padlock and used a key on the set he had taken from Turner to unlock it. He pushed open the gate and drove onto the property.

It began to rain, the drizzle falling in a fine mist. Eric fumbled to find the switch for the windshield wipers. The estate floated into view ahead like a grand cruise ship on a storm-tossed sea, studded with lights.

He decided to ditch the car and travel the rest of the distance on foot. Less chance someone might hear him approaching.

Turner had said he could reach the cellar via a service door located on the western side of the mansion, that he would recognize it because Lorenzo's Navigator would be parked there. Eric stashed the revolver in his right pocket and his phone in his other pocket and got out of the hearse.

Here we go.

He hurried through the cold drizzle, shoes crunching across gravel.

On the side of the house, he saw the Lincoln Navigator parked in a driveway that ended at a large set of double doors. A flood light glowed above the entrance.

His heart drummed as he got closer. If Lorenzo were in the SUV...

But the vehicle was dark, quiet. Eric arrived at the doors. Another key on Turner's ring opened them.

He crossed the threshold. He was a large vestibule, the walls lined with empty crates. A short flight of steps led upward, into the main section of the house. Another steep set of stairs descended into the cellar.

Downstairs, a series of recessed lights illuminated a bizarre spectacle: a long stone-floored corridor lined with portraits, inscriptions, and granite slots that looked like mail chutes.

The catacombs.

He shook off his queasiness and hurried along the hallway. Turner had said Destiny was being kept in a storage room. He prayed that they hadn't already deposited her in a crypt of her own.

He scanned the portraits as he half-walked, half-jogged down the hallway. A painting that looked eerily like Sonya Cannon brought him to a full stop.

Sonya was posed like the model in the *Mona Lisa*, lips curved in an enigmatic smile. He read the engraved inscription underneath the portrait:

Sonya, My Sweet Angel

Life took you too soon, but we will always remember you with fondness and love.

A thorn punctured his heart. He had barely known Sonya, but their lives had been inextricably joined in a bond that would outlast them.

He felt sorry for his daughter—their daughter—most of all.

Now find her.

On the other side of the corridor, he noticed a door. It was ajar, darkness thick beyond the threshold. He flipped the light switch beside the doorway and pushed the door open.

It was a storage room. A dozen cardboard boxes were stacked high as his head. On the other side of the room, he saw a thin mattress lying on the floor, like something you might find in a hastily arranged evacuee shelter.

But Destiny was gone.

53

Destiny awoke in a bedroom. In the pale light, she discovered that she lay on a real bed atop a frame, not a cheap mattress tossed onto a dusty floor. Her mind chugged slow as a clogged drain, but her memory upon waking this time was clearer than it had been earlier: they had drugged her again. She remembered the petite, flat-eyed woman who had slipped the syringe into her neck as easily as a tailor inserting a needle into a pin cushion.

As she blinked, Destiny smelled her own perspiration—*God, she needed a shower badly*—and cigarette smoke. She didn't smoke cigarettes. She raised her head off the embroidered pillow and saw a large, elderly Black woman sitting in a chair on the other side of the room.

The woman was well put together. Artfully applied make-up concealed her true age. Her hair was lustrous and black, threaded with a few streaks of gray—probably a high-quality wig. She wore a pricey-looking crimson dress, a pearl necklace, black pumps, and enough costume jewelry to fill a treasure chest.

The woman took note of Destiny as she tapped ashes from her cigarette into a gold ashtray.

"You're awake now, hmm?" She spoke in a throaty purr, like a satiated panther. "Good."

Destiny had never seen this woman before in her life, but she could see the faint resemblance in the eyes between her and the crazy guy,

Lorenzo. Was this Mama Cannon, the woman he'd spoken of with such reverence?

"Where am I?" Destiny asked.

"In your mother's bedroom. I thought it would be a kindness to let you see it."

Wincing, Destiny sat up. It looked like a bedroom from two decades ago that might have belonged to a teenager. The walls were painted a rich, coral hue, with white crown molding. A bookshelf held a collection of brown-skinned ceramic figurines. Posters of nineties-era romance films such as *Love and Basketball* and *Love Jones* were pinned to the walls.

"Where's my father?" Destiny asked. With a pang of anxiety, she remembered the man's scream she had heard earlier.

The woman spread her hands, as if her father had been scattered to the corners of the earth like leaves in a whirlwind. Destiny's heart lurched.

"Who are you?" Destiny asked.

The stranger indicated the room with a wave of her simmering cigarette. "Look around, child."

Destiny looked, saw a framed photograph standing on a white desk. A young woman and an older woman posed together in the picture, and the older woman bore an uncanny resemblance to the elderly lady sitting across from her.

"Are you my grandmother?" Destiny asked. She asked it flatly, like she would have asked about the weather forecast. She had no emotional connection to this woman. They shared DNA but they were strangers.

"No one has called me *grandmother* before." She spoke the word as if it were from a foreign tongue. "But it is what it is. Blood's a funny thing, isn't it?"

Destiny shrugged.

"I can see my baby girl in you," her grandmother said. "My sweet, broken girl. I never had much use for a daughter—daughters are a liability in this harsh world—but when she was a child, she was my heart, indeed she was."

Destiny pushed off the bed. She felt woozy for a spell and grabbed the bedpost to steady herself. She realized she was barefoot. Her sneakers were paired in front of a dresser.

Slowly, Destiny crossed to the desk and picked up the photograph. She traced her finger along her mother's face, her heart thumping.

My mother. Finally.

She was about Destiny's age in the photo, perhaps a little younger. An attractive young lady. She smiled in the picture, but there was a sadness in her soft eyes.

"What happened to her?" Destiny asked.

"What happens to broken things under pressure, inevitably." Her grandmother took a long pull on her cigarette and exhaled a column of smoke to the ceiling.

"Suicide?" The word felt like a stone in Destiny's mouth.

"Her actions brought shame down on our family, on me. I was competing with my siblings for control of the business and could not abide appearing like an incapable, foolish woman." She stared at Destiny, smoke shifting across her face. "I've had to earn my place in this world, even among my own family."

Her words, delivered in a matter-of-fact tone, gave Destiny a chill. She had to get out of here and away from these dangerous people, whether they were her mother's family or not.

"Can I go now?" Destiny asked. "I want to go home, please."

"Where is home, child?"

Destiny's response was automatic: "To my father." She swallowed, her dry throat clicking. "I never should have left his house in the first place. I was messed up in the head, I guess."

"You want to go home to your father now." Her grandmother smiled, as if amused at some private joke, and Destiny felt a ripple course through her stomach. Her grandmother gestured toward the door with her cigarette. "You see the door. But I think you ought to stay a while longer, sweetheart. I'm pleased with this conversation of ours." She flicked her tongue between her lips like a serpent tasting the air. "Hmm. I might have been wrong about you when you were a baby."

"You forced my mother to put me up for adoption," Destiny said. "Didn't you?"

"As I said, I had to fight for my place in my family. A squalling baby girl added nothing to my cause."

"That was it?" Destiny blinked back an unexpected rush of tears. "I would've made you look bad?"

"You're still a tender-headed child. I don't expect you to understand. Yes, we gave you away like a fruit basket." Her grandmother pantomimed dropping off a package. "I wrapped you up in a blanket, dropped you off at the front door of Grady Hospital in Atlanta, and left it in God's hands. Put a little notecard on you, too, so they'd know your proper birthday." She beamed at Destiny.

"It sounds like you did me a favor. Anything would have been better than living here with a family full of snakes like you."

Destiny had hoped the insult might wound the older woman, but her grandmother only chuckled.

"You've got grit, child. I like that. I advise you to stay. If you go out that door now, I can't promise you'll be safe. The baby boy has a terrible jealous streak." Her grandmother laughed again, lightly. "What do you say, child? Stay a while?" She cast her heavy-lidded gaze toward the doorway. "Or will you go out there and take your chances against my proud little lion?"

54

Although finding the empty storage room worried Eric, he was determined to search every room, every closet, every nook of this place for his daughter before he gave up hope.

"No stone unturned," he whispered to himself, like a mantra. "Let's keep moving, man. Let's go."

He saw another staircase at the end of the corridor. This was a tight spiral staircase that wound upward around a steel column. He hurried to it and ascended.

He rested one hand on the gun in his pocket as he climbed the steps. He had no idea what he would find up there.

He reached a closed door. He opened it slowly, hoping the hinges wouldn't creak.

The door swung open with a whisper, leading into a corridor. Muted light from ornate wall sconces glimmered on a hardwood floor.

There were four doorways in his immediate vicinity: two on his left, two on his right. Ahead, the hallway emptied into a grand dining room. Beyond the dining room doorway, he saw the house's main hall, which he remembered from his prior visit.

He didn't hear any voices or footsteps. Distantly, rain tapped against unseen windows. His racing heart boomed like gunfire in his ears.

He opened the door on his left. It was a half-bath with brushed gold taps; it was vacant. The next room on his left, enterable via an arched doorway, led into an immense gourmet kitchen with marble countertops and glittering copper pots and pans hanging from hooks. An open bottle of wine stood on the broad island.

He turned to his right. The door across from the kitchen opened into a walk-in pantry as spacious as the entire kitchen at Eric's house.

The other door was partly shut. Darkness lay beyond the threshold.

He nudged the door open with his shoulder. It was dark inside but looked like an office. A desk occupied the center of the room, dominated by a wide-screen monitor.

A young woman sat at the desk, her face bathed in silver light emitted from the screen. She focused on something on the display, a smile curving her lips; a pair of ear buds were nestled in her ears. She giggled at whatever she was watching, sipped from a pink straw buried in a tall glass. It looked like she was drinking chocolate milk.

Angel, Eric remembered. It was the woman who had sedated him.

Because of the position of her chair relative to the doorway, she didn't notice his observation of her. Eric slipped inside and sidled along the wall, flanking her.

She was watching cat videos on *YouTube*. She snickered and sipped her drink with childlike pleasure.

She was so giddy that he felt almost guilty about disturbing her. Keeping a bit of distance between them, he leaned forward and tapped her shoulder.

"Hey," he said.

She spun around in the chair. Recognition flared in her eyes. She hissed.

"Wait a second," he said. "I'm not here to hurt you."

She sprang off the chair and tried to boot him in the groin. Because Eric had kept his distance, her foot only grazed his thigh.

"Listen to me, dammit," he said. "Where's my daughter?"

She bared her teeth and rushed him. She was fast, but tiny. He outweighed her probably by sixty pounds. She hurtled into him like a cannonball, but she couldn't knock him over. He grabbed the collar of her shirt and flung her away.

As she fell backward, the back of her head rapped against the desk's edge. The glass of chocolate milk tipped over. She collapsed to the floor in a heap. Milk dribbled over the desk and plopped onto her face.

He hadn't wanted to hurt her, but she was knocked out cold. He doubted she would have volunteered any information anyway. Every member of this wicked family was set against him.

He left the office, passed through the empty dining room, and entered the main hall. He dug the revolver out of his pocket and let it hang at his side.

"Destiny!" he shouted. "Destiny, it's Eric, your father! Are you here?"

From her dead mother's bedroom, Destiny heard her father calling her. Her heart leaped.

"He's here!" Destiny said.

"That can't be." Her grandmother looked as stunned as if she'd been slapped. Fingers quivering, she extinguished her cigarette in the gold ashtray. "No, that's incorrect."

"I'm going home," Destiny said. "You and your psycho son can go to hell. My dad's here to get me."

With great effort, her grandmother started to rise from her chair. Destiny rushed past her and flung open the bedroom door. She was on an upper-level catwalk, near a railing. The walkway overlooked a vast open space below.

Wow, this house was *huge,* outrageously opulent. She really hadn't seen much of it until then.

These people on her mom's side were obviously rich, like Clive had promised they were. But she meant what she'd said to her grandmother: they were snakes. Damn their money. She didn't want them in her life.

"I'm up here!" Destiny leaned over the railing, searching for Eric below.

She saw her father come into the big room downstairs. Eyes wide, he pointed.

"Look out!" he said.

Before Destiny could turn, someone grabbed her.

Eric was so excited finally to see Destiny upstairs that he could not believe it was her. But his jubilation gave way to terror when Lorenzo seized her from behind.

"No!" Eric dashed toward the grand spiral staircase.

He felt as if he were running underwater, the air thick against his movements.

Destiny screamed and struggled. But Lorenzo was too big, too strong. He wrapped one arm around her waist and another around her neck. He tipped Destiny over the edge of the railing and held her suspended. She flailed her arms, her braids swinging.

It was at least a twenty-foot drop to the marble floor below.

Please, God, Eric thought. *Don't let him do it. Not after all we've been through. Please.*

Eric had the gun in his hands. His palms were slick with sweat. He pounded up the steps, taking them two at a time.

"Let her go!" Eric said.

"I can definitely oblige, old man," Lorenzo said. He sounded eerily calm; the almost-bored tone of a cold-blooded killer.

"Don't do it, baby boy." Mary Cannon emerged from a nearby room. "Please, put the girl down."

"What?" Lorenzo's face twisted into a murderous mask. "*You* care about her now, Mama? But she's nothing! She's illegitimate, she's nobody in this family!"

Heart in his throat, Eric finally arrived on the catwalk. Mary, Lorenzo, and his daughter were close, but he worried he couldn't reach them in time.

A choked sob escaped Mary. She dabbed at her shimmering eyes with a handkerchief.

"She's your sister!" Mary cried. "I've never told a soul. My sweet Sonya had twins . . . I kept you!"

The revelation froze Eric in place.

Twins? Sonya had given birth to a boy and a girl?

Lorenzo was his son?

Jesus, it can't be.

Lorenzo screamed. He hurled Destiny over the railing.

Eric pulled the trigger. The gun boomed.

Lorenzo staggered, blood blooming on his chest. He looked at Eric, his eyes full of disbelief. Mary caught him as he collapsed.

Numb with shock, Eric realized Destiny was screaming. He swung around.

She hadn't fallen to her death. She had snagged a big crystal chandelier on her way down. She had both hands on it, her arm muscles straining to hold her alight. But the fixture's supporting chain rattled and creaked under her weight, paint chips fluttering from the ceiling.

"Hang on!" Eric scrambled back down the staircase.

He wouldn't get down there fast enough to catch her. He knew it. He was too far away, and the support beam was weakening by the second.

Hang on, sweetheart.

As he rounded the newel post at the bottom of the stairs, he saw Deacon. Deacon pushed a sofa underneath Destiny.

"Hey there, young lady," Deacon said, ever polite. "I've got you."

The chandelier's support chain broke with a loud *snap*. Screaming, Destiny dropped about fifteen feet and landed on the couch cushions with a tremendous bounce. The chandelier smashed against the floor, crystal fragments flying in every direction.

Eric hustled over to the sofa, shoes crunching across the broken glass.

"I thought you might need a hand, Newton." Deacon winked.

Eric reached for Destiny, arms opened wide. She leaped off the couch and into his embrace.

"I'm sorry." She sobbed. "I'm so sorry."

Eric was crying, too.

"I'm sorry, too," he said.

Upstairs, Mary wailed.

57

Eight weeks later

"Sorry I'm late." Eric settled into the chair across from Destiny at the café in Little Five Points. "Traffic was terrible. We get a little drizzle and everyone in the city suddenly forgets how to drive."

"No worries, Dad." She put down the hardcover she was reading; it looked like another Octavia Butler novel. "I'm glad you could make it."

"You're the one with the busy schedule these days. I get in where I fit in."

"Whatever, man." Smiling, she slid a menu toward him, raised her coffee mug. "I'm drinking a latte. They're great, if you're a latte fan."

Eric scanned the menu, but his gaze kept skipping back to his daughter. She looked good; like a young woman with her whole life ahead of her. He couldn't have been prouder.

After the events in Grisby, Destiny had moved in with his family for about a month. Then, she and her cousin, Jalen, had decided to become roommates. They found a loft in the Old Fourth Ward in Atlanta. It was a perfect location for them. Jalen was a student at Georgia State, downtown; Destiny had decided to attend cosmetology school and work toward a career as a hair stylist. Eric insisted on covering the cost of tuition and a portion of her rent, and after some wrangling, she accepted his offer, though she reminded him that she had a part-time job and was quite capable of hustling to make ends meet if necessary.

She was so independent and headstrong, this child of his. But he had learned to accept her, on her own terms.

Acceptance had become a key word for him, in multiple ways.

Accepting that he'd unknowingly fathered *two* children. Accepting that one of those children, his son, was a homicidal psychopath. Accepting that he'd been forced to choose between them, and he had chosen his daughter—and that he would gladly do it again.

"Are the media hounds still sniffing at your door?" Destiny asked.

"They've moved on. They've got short attention spans."

His determination to find his daughter had exposed the Cannon's sordid business practices to the world, thanks to Deacon's listening device and especially, Maurice Turner, who was suddenly eager to spill everything to snag a plea deal. Turner revealed that the Cannons were engaging in their body broker enterprise regardless of whether the decedents or families had given consent; they forged permission documents and then sold the cadavers and body parts to a wide network of companies. They had been doing it for decades and earned millions.

Eric didn't know if they had sold off pieces of his granddad's cadaver, too. He had his well-founded suspicions—but realized he didn't want to know. Either way, it wasn't going to bring his granddad back.

The murders, however, had been a relatively recent development. Mary couldn't resist deploying the depraved talents of her grandson and criminally insane niece, Angel, to further the family business. *Clearing the books,* was what she called it during her police interviews. In the past two years, the duo had fatally poisoned over thirty residents of their nursing homes.

Lorenzo had lethally injected Grandma Nellie. The twisted young man had murdered his own great-grandmother, though he hadn't known it at the time.

"How are you sleeping?" Destiny asked. "Better?"

"I have good nights, and bad. You?"

"I keep seeing his face." She sipped her latte, grimaced as if it were too bitter. "I feel as if I should have known he was my twin when I first saw him, like via a psychic bond or something, you know?"

"I should have known he was my son."

"It's all so damned wrong." She closed her eyes for a beat, shrugged. "I don't think I'll ever understand why it all happened."

"But you'll live with it. We both will. A day at a time."

He reached across the table, grasped her hand. She gave him a bittersweet smile.

"Try the avocado wrap, Dad," she said. "It's my favorite thing here."

"Sounds good to me."

The father and daughter had lunch together.

ABOUT THE AUTHOR

Brandon Massey was born June 9, 1973 in Waukegan, Illinois. He currently lives with his family near Atlanta, Georgia. Visit his web site at www.brandonmassey.com to learn more and to sign up for his mailing list.